Published by
Mind's Eye Publications
985 Deborah Avenue
Elgin, IL 60123-1918

Cover Art by Paul "Mutartis" Boswell
Cover Lettering by Frank Coffman

MIND'S EYE

PUBLICATIONS

ISBN 978-1-7367114-1-5 // Trade Paperback
$15.00 US

ECLIPSE OF THE MOON

Speculative Poetry by
Frank Coffman

ECLIPSE OF THE MOON

Speculative Poetry by
Frank Coffman

Illustrations and Cover Art by

Mutartis Boswell

FRANK COFFMAN is a retired professor of college English, Creative Writing, and Journalism. His two previous collections of verse: *The Coven's Hornbook & Other Poems* and *Black Flames & Gleaming Shadows* have each received consideration for the Stoker Award for Poetry Collection from the Horror Writer's Association.

He is also a member of the Science Fiction & Fantasy Poetry Association, and founder and moderator of the Weird Poets Society Facebook group.

His recent collaboration with fellow speculative poet, Steven Withrow, *The Exorrcised Lyric* (Mind's Eye Publications, February 2021) offers two long narrative collaborations and 20 poems from each of the poets.

This third large collection of his work features more poems across the genres of the speculative, including especially the weird, horrific, and supernatural, but also inclusive of some science fictional and some more in the realm of fantasy and legend.

As with the first two poetry collections, this book also includes some metapoetry, some *hommages*, and some more "traditional" verse. Different in this tome are two large sections: *The Decipherment* (an *epyllion* [mini-epic]) in the Cthuluvian vein and a 111 sonnet sequence over 72 titles, *Sonnets for the Dead of Night* in the tradition of the *Weird Tales* sonnet sequencers: Donald Wandrei, H. P. Lovecraft, and Robert E. Howard.

Also included is an *Addendum* to his *Khayyám's Rubáiyát* featuring 72 quatrains for the forthcoming second edition of that work.

He lives in Elgin, Illinois, married to Connie. They are owned by two cats: Buffy (calico who slays vampires) and Binx (ghost chaser).

Dedications

For all **Singers of Tales** in the oral and derived traditions of myth and folklore and the high imagination: the chanters of epics, the bards, the skalds, the scops, the minstrels, the troubadours, and the balladeers.

For the **Sonnet Sequencers**: Petrarch, Dante, Spenser, Shakespeare, Sidney, Tuckerman, Wandrei, Lovecraft, Howard, Smith, Drake, Sidney-Freyer and all. And for all who have developed the quatorzain and established it as the perfect and ubiquitous "poetic paragraph."

For the **Old Tent Maker—Omar** and those who followed in his patterns, themes, and traditions, and for the many who have translated and recast his ruba'i into many tongues.

And for all my **Fellow Poets of The Speculative** across its several genres.

With special thanks to my "Partner in Rhyme," **Steven Withrow** for letting me "bounce off" his fine critical sense for comment so many of the poems herein—and, also, of course, for friendship.

Also with special thanks, to **Paul "Mutartis" Boswell** for his magnificent imaginings and distinctive talent and the resultant art and illustrations contained in this collection, so "in tune" with the essences of the words in my poems. "Hands (and Minds) Across the Sea." Cheers, Mate!

—F.C.

List of Illustrations by
MUTARTIS BOSWELL

Table of Contents

Table of Contents (cont.)

Table of Contents (cont.)

POET'S PREFACE

This is my third large collection of poetry. It follows *The Coven's Hornbook & Other Poems* (2019) and *Black Flames & Gleaming Shadows* (2020). As with these first two collections, the poems to be found herein primarily include work in the speculative genres of Horror & the Supernatural, Fantasy (especially mythic and legendary), and Science Fiction. Also, as in the first two volumes, there are later sections in the tome that fall under the headings of metapoetry (poetry about poetry itself and the writing of poetry) and another inclusive of a more "traditional" variety—at least verse that would not properly be subsumed within the nature of *the speculative*.

I have also included an *Addendum* to my 2019 book, *Khayyám's Rubáiyát*, in which I render a new version into English verse of quatrains from the Khayyámic tradition (since it is almost universally ageed among scholars that only about 75 to 100 of the quatrains are likely originals by the old "Tent Maker." These will also be included in my forthcoming second edition of that tome.

Two significant sections of the book are: first, a long narrative poem, *The Decipherment*, which I am calling an *epyllion* (a "mini-epic" of sorts); and, second, a long sequence of sonnets, *Sonnets for the Dead of Night*, inclusive of 72 titles, but—since several of the titles include short sets or sequences of sonnets within themselves—for 111 sonnets in total the full sequence is significantly larger. These sections are central to the book, with several speculative poems in a short section before them and the several Khayyámic quatrains, with metapoetic, *hommage*, traditional poems, and another handful of "supernaturals" and "horrific/weird" following.

As with the first two collections, I have included a "Glossary of Forms" at the back of the book. *This is not done in any attempt to insult the intelligence of those readers who already have a firm grasp on traditional metered and rhymed verse and verse forms or a solid grounding in the concepts of prosody. Rather, as with the first two collections, I am sim-*

ply clarifying the many traditional forms in Western tradition, but also the exotic, cross-cultural, experimental, and invented forms used in this collection. Experimental and invented forms are indicated by an asterisk*

I owe great debts of thanks to fellow poet and friend, and my "Partner in Rhyme," Steven Withrow (with whom I have collaborated on our recently published *The Exorcised Lyric* (February 2021) for his critical commentary and suggestions on many of the poems herein and, as always, both encouragement and useful opinions; and another debt of great thanks to my friend, the wonderful artist and illustrator, Paul "Mutartis Boswell," who, as with my collection *Black Flames & Gleaming Shadows* and the collaboration collection *The Exorcised Lyric*, has added his vision and unique talent to several amazing depictions based upon the content of my poetry. He has certainly captured the essence of my poetic concepts with his wonderful and distinctive illustrations.

My long-lived love of things mythic, epic, legendary, and folkloric—the "Bardic Tradition" in general—moved me to try my hand at the longer sustained narrative, *The Decipherment*. I have attempted to emulate an ancient Sanskrit meter in this blank verse poem that ranges from an archeological dig at Harappa in India, through Egypt, and thence to Easter Island. Boswell's amazing illustrations complement my verses remarkably well. His artistic visions in this "epyllion" hugely enhance the story that I attempted to set down in words.

As for the long sequence, *Sonnets for the Dead of Night*, I have said and written many times that I consider myself to be primarily a "sonneteer," although I attempt to explore formal poetry in many patterns across history, a variety of cultures and ethnicities, experiments, and innovations. But I consider the ubiquitous form of the sonnet the perfect "paragraph of verse," a little square upon the page that presents the primary challenges upon which poetry is grounded: compactness of expression, innovations of imagery, surprises of sound, and depth of thought and emotion presented more impactfully than prose can—with few exceptions—achieve.

Being also aware of the tradition of sonneteers inspired to create *sonnet sequences*, I thought I'd try my "Mind's Hand" (as my favorite Medieval rhetorican, Geoffrey of Vinsauf, so eloquently puts it in his *Poetria Nova* [ca 1200]) to the task of a sonnet sequence.

So, while it is certainly a bold move to follow the likes of Petrarch, Dante, Spenser, Sidney, Shakespeare, Milton—but, likely with more relevance, Wandreai, Lovecraft, Howard, Sterling, Smith, Drake, and Sidney-Freyer—I struggled with this labor of love for a collection of 72 titles and 111 sonnets. This was done not only as a challenge to myself, but certainly also as an *hommage* to these "sequencers" of the form who have established and carried on that tradition.

There are many exceptionally talented contemporary poets of *The Speculative*. And the market for poems—literature in general—across the genres of what I call the "High Imagination"—Adventure, Detection & Mystery, Fantasy, Horror & the Supernatural, and Science Fiction has never really waned.

As H. Rider Haggard wrote in his imporant essay, "About Fiction":

> "The love of romance is probably coeval with the existence of humanity. So far as we can follow the history of the world we find traces of it and its effects among every people, and those who are acquainted with the habits and ways of thought of savage races will know that it flourishes as strongly in the barbarian as in the cultured breast. In short, it is like the passions, an innate quality of mankind....
>
> [A "refuge" from the relatively new genres of Naturalism and Realism] lies in the paths and calm retreats of pure imagination. Here we may weave our humble tale, and point our harmless moral without being mercilessly bound down to the prose of a somewhat dreary age. Here we may even—if we feel that our wings are strong enough to bear us in that thin air—cross the bounds of the known, and, hanging between earth and heaven, gaze with curious eyes into the great profound beyond.
>
> There are still subjects that may be handled there if the [writer] can be found bold enough to handle them. And, although some there be who consider this a lower walk in the realms of fiction, and who would probably scorn to become a "mere writer of romances," it may be urged in defence of the school that many of the most lasting triumphs of literary art belong to the producers of purely romantic fiction..."

Why my emphasis on "Fiction" and the focus of Haggard's quote? It is because I firmly believe that the focus of speculative literature—especially speculative poetry with which I am primarily concerned—should be on the Narrative and what we might call the "Atmospheric-Descriptive" modes of poetry. I would add to that the Dramatic and, to a degree (especially relevant in Science Fiction and Fantasy), the Didactic modes. This is not to say that the Lyric has no place in the poetry of the speculative.

I am trying to write my verses (and the short fiction that I also work with) in the tradition of the classic *Weird Tales* poets and authors—thinking of the traditions of "The Pulps" in general.

As the reader will discover—in case you don't know some of my work already—I am a Formalist, a writer of traditional verse forms, with the great majority of my poems being in rhyme and meter. Those are, indeed, "traditional" *Containers*. What I believe you will discover herein, and in all of my poetic work, are the distinctly "non-traditional" *Contents*....Yet, in another important sense, as Haggard notes regarding the ubiquity of a "love of Romance," my work is actually very *Traditional* in the sense of the topics and themes falling under the several genres of *Popular Imaginative Literature*, which, as I see it, are merely extensions of the Mythic, the Legendary, and the Folkloric (what we may call "Illiterature"—highly imaginative tales and traditions from the age of "Oral Culture" [as Fr. Walter Ong has termed it] carried into the Age of Print. Those types of themes and tales are, as Haggard terms it, "coeval with the existence of humanity."

— Frank Coffman, Elgin, Illinois, Vernal Eqinox 2021

Miscellaneous Macabres, Monstrosities, & Misnaturals

A Thin Place

I remember well that day Professor Quinn,
In an early lecture in that elective course—
The Paranormal: An "Out There" Introduction
(Delivered with the old gent's typical force)—
About how there were places that were…"Thin":

"Places and zones in this—the world we know—
Where the barrier between our 'real' realm and the next
Is tenuous at best; where the 'normal' obstruction,
'The Veil,' is pellucid or torn. Such points are hexed,
And movement between such spheres may freely flow."

Of course, I took the notes down—for the test.
Just a course title that grabbed me—sounded "fun"
At first. …But, as the weeks went swiftly on,
Through that—my last semester—I had begun
To develop this wonderment that would not let me rest.

I stayed for grad work in archeology
But did self-studies—both obscure and arcane—
Reading some nights straight through until the dawn,
Seeking a solution both rational and sane
To that quandary that Quinn had made me see.

* * *

So it surprised me greatly when our guide
To this most strange, newly-discovered site
Deep in these foliage-dimmed Honduran hills
Said, "This place is 'Thin.' We must leave before the night!
This place is 'Wrong!' Things from the 'Other Side'

Can see us here! And I fear can come 'Across!'"
   With skepticism, of course, even with some derision
From others in my team. But it gave me chills.
And, of course, we've already made the firm decision
To set up camp. *But Manuel signed the cross!*

2

"I beg you sirs, and madam, you must not stay!
[Jane, my wife, and I met three years before
At a dig at Saqqarah, a newly discovered tomb],
"This place is too near a 'Gate,' an open 'Door!'
Ah well, I'm going now. You know the way."

Before he left us, I asked Manuel to say
Exactly what he'd meant by his word: "Thin?"
His trembling answer, warning me of doom,
Was the same defined long years before by Quinn.
Our guide was long gone before the end of day.

* * *

Odd noises were all around us through last night—
Our first in this camp Manuel told us not to set.
The dig has turned up curiosities
That don't seem "right?" One thing I shan't forget:
A small idol carved of onyx—a thing of fright!

A round, cephalopodic, huge-eyed head
Atop a body lion-like and lean,
Yet scaled, reptilian, bat-winged. Monstrosities
Of all the ancient cultures I have seen,
But this thing fills me with a sense of dread.

* * *

So busy with the dig—it's now day three,
But I'll take just a little time to write.
We've certainly discovered something new—
Or, rather, old—too old! This eldritch site
Was built in some remote pre-history,

Far older than prior theory had expected!
Preliminary tests say fifteen-thousand years!
Some culture here was born and throve and grew.

3

Then—suddenly—was gone. The landscape bears
Signs of cyclopean structures, long neglected.

And Smythe says DNA beneath some stones
Are specimens from some yet unknown creature!
Last night, I saw a strange light through the trees,
And, recalling the cryptic words of my old teacher,
I searched awhile, but no 'Gate' between zones

Was there to find. And so, I'm here at camp.
Jane is asleep, Mitchell and Smythe are snoring.
One more note: There's a stench upon the breeze
I've never smelled before. I'll go exploring
After dawn, but I'll not chance it with a lamp.

* * *

"Have you seen Smythe?" Mitchell asked when we arose—
This our fourth morning here at "Lugar Delgado"
(As Manuel had called it—and so we kept the name)
We've looked about. But, so far, we don't know
Where the Hell he's gone? My apprehension grows,

But I don't want to share my thoughts with Jane
Or Mitchell. At least not yet. Not 'til I'm certain
My fears are justified. But how to frame
What I suspect: We're near to a frail 'Curtain'
Between two worlds! They'd both think I'm insane.

* * *

We've found no sign of Smythe. We searched all day.
Not even an echo met our constant cries.
We've decided to head back to the Rio Platano
When morning comes. But now this long day dies.
Mitchell is shaken....The first time I've seen Jane pray.

4

* * *

It was not yet dawn. Mitchell woke us—screaming!
We left our tent. And there, across the glade
The "Gateway" gleamed. In horror, we saw him go
Into a glowing mist no good god made.
And *They* were there! *Hideous!* but sentient-seeming!

We fled, ran quickly down the southwest slope,
Until we've come a good mile from our tent.
Here in this jungle's lush dark undergrowth,
We'll shelter. But we know this zone is…"bent."

* * *

Now dawn. We'll move on. One more day and night and—Hope.

* * *

Just one more night. We've come at least halfway
Back to the settlement. I'll find Manuel!
God! He was right—and Quinn! Things we both
Have glimpsed through that open "Doorway to Hell!"
Things beyond frightening, terrible, fell, and fey!

* * *

I'm writing this five hours before a dawn
That I will never see. The tales are true!
There are places where the "worlds" aren't separate,
Where *They* can cross—*Things* so unlike me and you.
First Smythe, then Mitchell, and now Jane is gone!

* * *

Ah! Now it's time for my own reckoning!
If you find this journal, think whatever you please.
I see the glow! It's growing! Yes—"The Gate"
Is opening there, just past the nearest trees!
And *They* are here! And Jane is beckoning.…

The Ankou
(a sonnet in Breton Couplets)

Skeleton stark in grim dark shroud,
Shadowy form like a storm cloud,
An Ankou demon may be seen,
Seeking for new sad souls to glean.
Death's Henchman—this dire tale is spread—
In fell cart he gathers the dead,
Or black coach rolls, filled with souls he
Is cursed to grab to be set free.

Each year the last of the vast dead
Becomes this thing for the coming year.
All of the lost this wight most weird
Will harvest. He is rightly feared.
Seeing this wight 'neath the bright moon,
Know that one more sees Death's door soon.

Dusk Dangers, Strange Seasons

(a sonnet in Telesilleans*)

The grey day into night descends;
The last light from the world's edge wends.
And now *Those* who would vex us here
May come forth and draw awfully near.
The Dark Veil is more easily rent
And fell Powers to our world are sent!
When day fades and our zone is dark.
The Weird Wights of the night embark.

Thus fey folk—though some disbelieve—
Are real banes. And some sure will grieve.
The Gate is wide on some special nights:
All Hallows' one with a feast of frights;
Yes, Samain and other Quarters roll...
Each Sun Point—there will be a toll.

Frank Coffman

Breed Accursed

(a Tercetina Sonnet, invented form*)

Around these somber rows of incised stones
In this old graveyard as harsh autumn cools
The land, there lurks a horrid, hell-born breed.

Foulest of all foul fiends, their gruesome need
Is violation of the dead, eat flesh, gnaw bones!
Abhorrent harvest, breaking all Nature's rules.

Ass-hooved, wolf-jawed, they are the Ghouls!
Loathsome they live and blasphemously feed,
Coming forth nightly from their nether zones.

Wind moans o'er chill pools. Take thee heed!

Yes, there are horrors worse, by far, than Death—
Despoilers of the hoped-for quiet grave
Breathe from foul maws their pestilential breath
After feasting on the curséd food they crave.

The Jiangshi

(a Chinese Chueh-Chu Sonnet* in an approximation of
Ch'i-Yen-Shih Meter*)

Fear you the dark! The Jiangshi,
Revenant fiends, roam the night;
Seek they for blood, vampiric
Zombies most dread. Such a fright
Seeks out live souls, feeds on flesh.
On our world they are a blight.
Visage of Death! But you might
Mistake them. They are bedight
In regal robes.
                           From behind
They seem human. But to view
The horrid face—corruption!
Decay and rot! Stark white grue!
Then far too late you will know
Its next victim…will be You!

All Hallows' Eve
(a sonnet in Dróttkvætt meter*)

All Hallows' Eve. Hurry, harry the still-living,
Fell foes with Hell's fury, freely roaming, laughing,
As mortal man, failing, most feebly to resist,
Potent attacks prevailing. Powers they might enlist
Are oft too long delayed. The Might of great Mages,
Some strong enough, indeed, schooled from the secret pages
Of grand grimoires, able, through lost incantations
When the World is unstable, to win o'er *Mis-creations*.

Terrors, *The Veil* tearing, travel in our demesne.
Hostile the Host bearing Horrors of Halloween.
Legion of Evil laughing, at the Lost who disbelieve.
Most mortals keep scoffing; for many—no reprieve.
Wicked wights all wending—when that *Great Gossamer* tatters—
Into Our World, sending such *Things* our sanity shatters.

Frank Coffman

The "Canni-Ballad" of Sawney Bean

(a sequence of Folk Ballad-Sonnets, invented form*)

There is a rocky headland jutting
  Into the Firth of Clyde.
Southwest, on Scotland's rocky coast,
  A dread clan did abide.

The patriarch, one "Sawney" Bean,
  With "Black Agnes" his consort
(Surnamed Douglas, a very witch)
  To murder did resort.

But worse than murder—always foul!—
  After those sins were fresh,
Sawney and Agnes and their ilk
  Had a taste for human flesh!

Tripling their curse: murder, man-flesh fed,
Their spawn increased by incest bred!

Yes, they were cannibals as well as thieves
  And killers in cold blood.
They'd take their victims to a cave
  Deep by the ocean's flood.

There they dismembered each grim corpse
  And boil or broil the bones.
They throve upon those grisly feasts
  Served up on table stones.

Eight were their sons, their daughters six,
  In Sawney's evil brood.
With thirty-two grandchildren born—
  All fed on unholy food.

13

The scattered bones strewn on the strand—
Deemed animal predation—as they'd planned.

For long the locals assumed as much,
    But then: "No!" they cried, "much deeper!"
"'Tis murder plain! Who saw them last?"
    They lynched a poor innkeeper!

And then another, and yet one more
    Who kept an hostelry,
Were hanged despite any evidence,
    Despite each innocent plea.

Then, one day coming home from a fair,
    A couple met attack
By Sawney, Agnes, and their cursed spawn—
    But the husband, brave, fought back.

Wounded, to save his wife he'd fail,
But he survived to tell the tale.

Word made its way to good King James
    Who sent four-hundred men
Along with bloodhounds to seek them out—
    All those who'd commit such sin.

They tracked them to that tidewater cave,
    They found all without fail.
They brought that clan to Edinburgh
    To sit in Tolbooth Gaol.

Justice was swift, all of the men—
    As to the damned befalls—
Their hands and their feet were removed;
    And knives took cocks and balls.

They spared the women not. They'd make
Them watch—then burned them at the stake.

An so the legend of Sawney Bean
  And the witch, Agnes the Black,
Ended with gruesome penalties—
  Of lessons there was no lack.

All ye who would defy God's laws,
  'Gainst murder, incest—and worse!
Those who'd partake of human flesh
  Will suffer an awful curse.

Yet Sawney and his Godless brood—
  1000 Lives were lost!—
Survived for years on ghoulish food
  Before they paid the cost.

Yet 'tis well that clan of fiends now dwell
Forever in the depths of Hell.

Lycan

(using Clark Ashton Smith's form from his poem "Zothique")

He who survives the werewolf's baleful bite
Is transformed on the next month's full moon night.
There is no remedy for this vile curse—
Or the *Thing* he must become!
And neither man nor wolf—but something worse
Will plague the countryside.

He who has seen the wound fade fast, turn white,
And seen *the pentagram* (as it is hight)
Appear there in its place—that man will change!
No hope! He must succumb
On full moon nights—a monster: heinous, strange,
All Nature's laws defied!

He who transforms into this wicked wight
Will often not remember in daylight
What he has done 'neath Luna's glowing face.
There may be only some
Dim memory, if chancing upon the place
Where his own victim died.

He seeks some way to end his horrid plight,
But, finding none, he knows when the moon is bright
And at the full, he'll wend out craving flesh.
There's no escaping from
That change where beast and man will mesh!
As he stalks far and wide.

The Greyman of Ben MacDhui
An Old Scot Tells a Tale
(Folk Ballad form)

"We Scots who live 'neath Ben MacDhui
  Know that a fearsome horror
Haunts that high mountain in the Cairngorm.
  A thing known as *Am Fear Liath Mor.*

"Tales tell the Greyman of Ben MacDhui
  Stands nearly ten feet high!
And if ye see him, dim through the gloom,
  Ye'd better turn and fly!

"Some scoff: 'He's just a trick of light,
  A shadow on frost mist,
Mistaken for a giant beast.'
  But to my story list!...

"I walked upon those darkling crags
  One evening long ago.
At first, I felt a sense of dread.
  I swear to you 'twas so!

"But then, a dark shape in the fog,
  Far taller than a man,
Emerged and came full into view—
  Imagine, if you can!

"A huge, grey-furred—yet manlike—thing,
  A stench that was most foul,
And though the wind was up that eve,
  'Twas drowned out by its howl!

"I saw it clear—and it saw me
  With eyes of fiery red!
I count myself no cowardly man.
  But I screamed—and turned—and fled.

"I tell you that the legend's true
  The Greyman haunts MacDhui.
No thing of shadow is *Liath Mor*—
  But alive! as you and me.

Frank Coffman

The Hidebehind:
A Legend of the North Country
(Split Couplets*)

Our Forests teem with things to fear—
And some come near.

Of course the wolf and Grizzly Bear
Can be found there.

And cougars to West and angered moose
In East are loose.

But there are some, to most unknown—
From a different zone.

A thing that lives in Northern Wood,
Takes folk for food!

The legend warns all those who stray
Past light of day.

The tales all tell a ferocious beast
Will have a feast.

For human flesh—its favorite food!
It craves man's blood!

It is well known some lumbermen
Don't return again.

And yet no one can tell its shape.
For few escape.

The thing will hide behind a tree
So none can see.

Concealed by boulder it will lurk—
Then do its work!

Some say—who've lived—a sense of Fear
Grows when it's near.

But all insist it has a knack
To be in back!

Intestines are it's favorite part!
Sometimes the heart!

And all too oft remains are found
Upon cold ground.

So nights—though not logging—lumberjacks
Carry their axe.

But most, from the warm fire of the stove,
Refuse to rove.

Far better to be wary and not find
The Hidebehind.

Dog Star

(a Fibonacci*)

Bright
"Dog Star,"
Sirius,
and Orion's belt—
why are they always so easy
to spot when we gaze?
Long ago,
were they
Home?

The Blue Holes of Andros
Two Bahamian Legends
(a nonce form)

On and around Andros trifurcated[1] isle
The Blue Holes beckon divers who would dare
To search their depths. But all such should beware
What lies within those sea-linked ink-dark caves.
The natives know the Lusca[2] dwells down there
And know, for those who meet it, nothing saves
Their reckless life. The great-toothed jaws,
The tentacles—against all Nature's laws!—
That giant horror means Death!
                                    Meanwhile
The owl-like, weird Chickcharney[3] haunts the wild,
Surrounding groves and thickets. Those beguiled
Who treat the creature well will be long-blessed,
But those who dare to laugh or to mistreat
That red-eyed, three-toed thing will suffer long,
Their life by constant ills and woes distressed,
Their lot to know a living Hell complete.

Mere Caribbean legends, a folk plainsong?
No! Two beasts plague that weird and wondrous place:
One like a bird of prey with prehensile tail,
A trickster thing that can be bane or boon,
There in the forest pines that hide the moon;
The other a huge cephalopodic shark,
A threat to all who swim, to all who sail
Over blue waters…but the depths are dark!
A Thing of the hidden horrors of *Inner Space.*

NOTES: on "The Blue Holes of Andros"

[1] The Bahamian "Island" of Andros is actually an archipelago, consisting of hundreds of small islets and cays connected by mangrove estuaries and tidal swamplands, It is comprised of three major islands: North Andros, Mangrove Cay, and South Andros. These three main islands are separated by "bights," estuaries that trifurcate the island, connecting the island's east and west coasts.

[2] The Lusca is a creature of Caribbean folklore, known throughout the many islands that are contained within the Bermuda Triangle. Bahamian folklore connects it most directly with the "Blue Holes" (roughly 175 on the island and 25 offshore) that connect to a sub-marine, sub-terrestrial system of caves, most of which have not been explored. Most accounts say that it is a hybrid monster with the head of a shark with a tentacled body like an octopus or squid. It is said to be as large as 75 to 200 feet in length.

[3] The Chickcharney is reputed to be an owl-like creature with a prehensile tail, red eyes (or one red eye) and three toes on each foot. This mischievous trickster lives in the thick pine forest and mangrove thickets of Andros and can bestow either blessings or curses upon those who encounter it.

THE DECIPHERMENT:
AN EPYLLION

27

THE DECIPHERMENT
(An Epyllion)

[in an English approximation of Sanskrit Drutavilambita Meter[1]
as used by Kalidasa and Deokota]

Prologue:
*The Warning Page Wrapped Around a Scroll
within a Chest in the Sepulcher
of Daniel Francis Chapman, PhD.
Haythorne Cemetery, Arkham, Massachusetts*

*Hidden inside this old chest bound with iron bands
Is a true tale that recounts a discovery—
How a rare find led to Horror and Death. It tells
Of the decipherment—terrible, yet true—of two
Scripts that were lost to the Ages it seemed. But found
To be most dreadfully linked! And this tale itself
Is a great danger to read, for it just might lead
Others to follow the path that we took and look
Further into the vile secrets discovered. Don't!
Don't for the sake of your Life—of our World!—explore
The eldritch language indexed by those glyphs! For doom
Lies in this greatest discovery that must die
Along with me. Let this story turn into dust
Just as will I who should never have set it down.
Yet some weird Power compelled it be written!
I can but warn that the secrets herein might bring
Such horrid Darkness—to turn this our Earth to a Hell
Far worse than any imagination could hold.
Dear Soul, forebear to read on! You've been warned…
 You've been told!*

The Tale of the Decipherment:
MMS Journal of Daniel Francis Chapman, PhD.

That noon the sun was unmerciful, breathing hot
Over the last day of our dig at Harappa,
High in the cloudless blue, it hung like an angry Eye....
    But when my trowel uncovered the shards. I knew—
To my astonishment—what we'd been seeking was found!
In unmistakable clarity, glyphs! And not
In a small grouping as normally found. But these!—
Here there were hundreds arranged in neat rows. And more!
    There was diversity shown. Very few repeats!
Oh, there were some repetitions but, clearly, here
Was an extended and—finally!—worthy script,
More than the cryptic brief snatches of various shapes
That had so mystified scholars for these many years.
    A few more strokes with my brush and more figures appeared!
It had been broken in two, but the passage was whole!
Here were enough of the Indus weird glyphs to begin
The task: deciphering what had been lost—the great,
Perhaps the greatest, epigrapher's challenge. Now
It might be possible that ancient tongue to know!

* * *

    That night I placed both the pieces together. There
On the camp table just under the lantern's light.
Sitting beside me both Smith and Petrovich looked on.
All of us beamed, for we knew just how wondrous a find
Lay on that table before us. It could prove the key!
Petrovich wanted to use some obscure algorithm;
And as was usual, Smith said, "We need a biscript[2]

Nothing can come if we don't have a parallel—
Text for comparison. There's no Rosetta key
Such as the Greek that assisted Champollion
When he deciphered the Ancient Egyptian glyphs."
   "But we at least know a little about the signs,"
I had remarked—yes, perhaps, it was wishful thought.
"Here is a corpus of glyphs, and the largest found
Up to this point. And we might just assume the tongue,
Based on the region, is likely to be a form…
Some form of Indo-Iranian[3], or at least
One of the older Proto-Indo European[4]—
Certainly older, perhaps even far older
Than classic Sanskrit a tongue we know well. Yet still,
If there's no progress along, those lines of thought, we might
Go to the ancient odd forms of the Arabic,
Or take great leaps! We might try the Egyptian
As some have done, even seeking comparisons
Between those ideographic known signs and these
That we've discovered. Or even Sumerian?—
Although those latter are wildly unlikely—But here!…
Here, on this table before us, we have—a start!"
   "Fine, but we certainly won't have it solved tonight,"
At that we smiled. Good old Petrovich laughed out loud,
For his wry comment was patently true, of course.
   "We cannot argue with that, my friend, Igor," said Smith.
   "Yes, it is late, and I know we're all weary," I said.
"It's nearly two, and we all need the rest."
                                  Yet I
Was very sure that no sleep would be mine that night,
That I would spend those dark hours deep in thought. Morning
Would see the dawn of my quest, my long-sought reward.

Many had scoffed at us three in our ten-year search.
But now these fragments of pottery could prove key
To the discovery of a thus-far unknown race....
To a strange culture that had weirdly disappeared.

* * *

   In the dim grey of the dawn, I awoke and went
Across our large tent to the box where we'd placed the shards,
Carefully cushioned on cotton and swathed in cloth.
The folds of linen I opened, revealing
The finely painted designs—what a mystery here!
For nearly all of that script that had been—at least
Thus far discovered—were worked into clay. Yet here,
There were not only clear glyphs, but in bright shades wrought?
The ancient pigments had kept their original hues!
Here there were blood-reds and yellows and greens—along
With the crisp black in which most had been drawn. But more—
Far more important the number of signs! This proved,
Beyond any doubt that the glyphs glossed a written tongue.
There had been some who even doubted they were writing:
Only mere art like the Göbekli Tepe[5] shapes.
But the sheer number of lines and of signs was proof.
This was a text! And a language lay waiting there.
And, perhaps, finally we had a place to start.
Previous work had already succeeded in showing
That, if it were a writing system at all,
It must be read from the right to the left. Although
A very scant few examples were boustrophedon[6]—
In which the signs and the reading would be reversed
In each succeeding line: thus, reading left to right
And with the curious mirroring of the glyph shapes.

Here it appeared that the signs were all right to left.
And it was generally thought—based on 400 glyphs—
That it was neither an *alphabet*[A], nor a type,
Due to that number, of some form of *syllabary*[B].
There were too few of the glyphs to be *logographs*[C].
No way in Hell! For example, the Chinese forms—
Over ten-thousand of those to be mastered!
And after that, every sign had many meanings.

　　No. I was sure that the script was *logo-syllabic*[D].
Some of these glyphs were whole words and some syllables.
But just what language they indexed? Unknown—"For now,
But we will find out the answer. There must be a way."
Of the new signs there were some that were curious:
One was cephalopod—octopus? squid? I thought
It a bit strange, since Harappa and "The Mound of the Dead"—
Mohenjo Daro—were both miles from the sea.
The other was circular. But very strange. It had
Multiple dots, many spots within a circle?
"Perhaps they had pizza," I grinned. "Pepperoni?"
Another glyph—was like a bat with outspread wings.
And one was beastial, a hybrid of creatures odd.

* * *

　　Within a few minutes both Petrovich and Smith were there.
And it was Smith who excitedly said, "We might
Consider tables like Ventris used working on
Linear B?" But I quickly responded, "No—
We cannot know the base language most likely here.
Linear B was quite clearly a syllabary,
With the addition of *rebuses*[E] and a few
Never-disputed clear *ideograms*[F]. Besides,

He had good reason to think it was Greek, though Greek
In a most primitive form. But his gridwork and charts?—
They could not serve to elicit the language here.
We've over four hundred signs. And these shards have some
We've never seen! At least three dozen more are here!"

    "Might we not guess that it's Proto-Dravidian[7]?" said
Igor Petrovich. "At least that's a place to start?"

    "To me it seems more akin to the patterns seen
In the Egyptian. Perhaps determinant[8] word signs
Are here admixed with the sound signs as syllables?"
This I suggested. To which they both seemed to agree.
The one thing sure was the lack of a starting point.
With no bilingual comparison text, the task
Seemed insurmountable. Back to the books we went.

* * *

    I know not what took me back to that paper—the one
I had regarded as foolishness, but I read
Once more de Devesy's wildly strange theory
That he had published far back in the 30s: How,
Strangely, quite similar many an Indus glyph
Seemed near identical to Rapa Nui's "Talking Wood."

    "This is, of course, quite impossible!" I told myself.
The two are thousands of years and vast distance apart."
Then I remembered Thor Heyerdahl's raft journey.
That crew had braved the Pacific—proven it could be done!
I looked again at the charts of the parallel glyphs.
"Yes, there is something here," I said to myself.
The more I looked at the figures before me, I knew
That the odd signs of far distant Easter Island,
Carved into wood—the strange *Rongorongo*—

These were, indeed, far too close for coincidence!
    At first, both Smith and old Petrovich had laughed
When I suggested we go to that far-off place.
    "You can't be serious," Smith said, and Igor agreed.
    But, when I showed them the charts, the comparable glyphs—
Just how, in row after row, near identical
Figures were found. First the Russian, then Smith concurred:
    "I am amazed, but, my friend, I must say you're right.
We have to go."
                        "Yes, but may I suggest Egypt first,"
Added Smith. "For we've already noted some hints
That the new text we have found is most likely close
To the Egyptian *phonetic-logographic* glyphs.
And we know experts there who might give advice."
    "I must agree with you there. And I also think
That we should write to von Junzt at Arkham's college.
He and his library at Miskatonic might
Offer some insights which we've yet to delve," I said.

* * *

And so we planned to set off the next day. Egypt—
And then to Chile whose distant territory,
That remote place, Rapa Nui, was a long plane ride from land,
Whose famed stone heads, the wide-eyed moai,
Eternally gazed. But at what we knew not—*but would learn!*

* * *

    When we arrived in old Cairo, we were met by Omar—
My old friend from my days in the Valley of Kings
Aiding in research into KV55[9] (which I still
Think is the tomb of great Akhenaten, condemned

35

For his new monotheistic views, his tomb
Sullied by priests who brought back the old pantheon).
But, though I knew hieroglyphics quite well, and Smith
Was near as skilled and accomplished as Omar,
Our task was not to do more Egyptology—
Rather to ask just what Omar thought of the theory
That our new shards showed a language that might compare
At least in kind to the Ancient Egyptian.

    After congratulating us on our find, he scanned
The script o'erwrit on the two shard segments. He paused
Briefly, then said,
               "I believe you are right, my friends.
I would say definitely *logo-syllabic, but linear*—
Unlike Egyptian artistic shapes that are bunched.
No glyphic stacking of forms is on these shards displayed.
And I agree that the lines read from right to left;
Note the clear crowding of glyphs on the left margin—
Some where the scribe did not plan well enough ahead—
Also we see that the lines are all flush on the right;
What gaps appear in the lines—they are all on the left.
This is a great, a quite wonderful find, my friends.
But I must note that I don't have the faintest clue
What these lines say. But I think you have taken steps
Toward your goal—that of finally breaking this code."

* * *

    Of course, we spent that first night near the pyramids,
Orion's Belt swinging through the black welkin—
Those huge monuments *spaced like those stars above!*
In awe we pondered the depth of the cosmos. What lay

Past our poor ken in those distant regions? Who knew
That our own journey would find some dark answers!
How could we know what the depths of that sky concealed?
How could we guess *the stark truths* that would be revealed?

* * *

With the next morning we found that a letter had come.
It had been sent to the home of our friend Omar,
Hoping to catch us before we departed Egypt.
Before we set off for Chile—and thence—Rapa Nui.
Doctor von Junzt, in great haste, had responded.
Our recent queries regarding the esoteric,
Curious tomes that were kept in that wondrous collection
(*There at Arkham in Miskatonic's room of rare books*)
Had more than piqued a keen interest in what we sought.
But we were shocked at the cautioning tone therein!
It was, indeed, a stern warning advising us
Not to depart, not until we had read the files
That he was sending in a separate posting.

"My friends, I cannot admonish you enough
To take great care if you go on this venture.
Please do not leave on your journey before reading
Files I am gathering. Yes! You are onto something.
For I have long understood a connection
Between the Indus inscriptions and those we see
In the reverse boustrophedon⁹ of Rongorongo.
But I have recently made a connection to
The horrid language that these signs might index.
There are some passages in Abdul Alhazred,
In the most rare tome we have here in Arkham—

Which only I and my student, young Dexter,
Are allowed to peruse in seclusion. That book
In itself is a danger to read.
                                    But, my friends,
In that dread book, the infamous Necronomicon,
Found by my namesake, my great grandfather,
These many years ago who, while in Damascus,
That tome discovered and secreted back to Arkham.
There is clear evidence that both those scripts are cursed!
Both the Harappan strange tongue and that of the island
That you intend to visit in your quest for fame.
    But, since I know that you three will continue
On with this quest I must ask you to seek out my friend—
Himself the great grandson of Metoro, who claimed
He could interpret the Rongorongo strange signs,
He who had worked with Tahiti's Bishop Jaussen
To attach meanings to various glyphs. My friend
Claims he has found more examples of "Talking Wood."
    In an excitedly wild and curious letter
That I received only weeks ago, he maintains
That there are other and terrible symbols—
Things that appear on this newly-found blade of an oar.
He is the only true expert on Rongorongo,
And I must urge that you seek my friend out as soon
As you reach Easter Isle, and show him the shards
That you discovered in distant Harappa.
And rest assured that—whatever he tells you—
That you may trust what he says to be true. Take care,
If you proceed with this journey for I have fear—
Fear that the danger is most grave—but for now I have
Only the inkling that my suppositions are true.

If they are true, then great Evils are threatening,
Not only you—but our world as a whole! There are,
From the deep cosmos, vile eldritch entities—
That long ago were expelled. But they threaten
A dread return—nay! a reawakening!
Be very wary, you three. Find Metoro
Seek out his wisdom and aid on this quest. I remain
Your old colleague and friend — Friedrich von Junzt.

* * *

"What an utterly strange correspondence," I said.
"We know he's always been oddly involved, in things
In that strange realm of the praeternatural. But this?"

"I think von Junzt has his own agenda on this,"
Said Horace Smith. "In this letter it's clear that he—
And, likely, this Metoro—are hoping to solve
The Indus riddle and earn that great credit
As well as praise for deciphering Rongorongo."

"Well, I don't think that von Junzt is that devious.
And he has never been other than helpful, Smith.
I must believe that his warning is serious."

"I must agree here with Smith's position."
Igor Petrovich commented. And then he said,
"We must at least be aware in that desolate place.
It's so remote—far from any potential help
From the mainland—over two thousand miles from Chile!"
Only a few of Earth's islands are as distant
From a substantial, inhabited mass of land...
Whatever truth there might be in von Junzt's words."

"Yes, we should rightly be as cautious as curious
And proceed on our quest with great care," I said.

* * *

40

On the next morning, we flew to Santiago,
Thence to charter a plane for the long shuttle
To distant Easter Island, far out to the West.
    Once we were off on that leg, the Pacific below us
Was anything but as "peaceful" as that name defines.
For we could see that the waters below us were roiling,
With the whitecaps whipped up by a typhoon below.
And a torrential rain nearly kept us from landing,
The small plane skidded a bit. Then we all breathed a sigh.
    There was one figure—drenched—waiting near the airstrip.
As we debarked, he came forward with outstretched hand.
"I am Metoro," he said "I am glad you are safe,
For the gods of the Sea *and* the Land must be angry."
    Just then a lightning bolt crashed into the volcano
Off to the southwest it also lit up some heads
Of some stern faces of Moai, standing silent,
Near to the landing strip. We'd only seen photos
Of those strange figures of stone, but they appeared—
By the fierce forks of the lightning to seem alive!
They seemed to gaze down on us with a knowledge
(With a weird wisdom we would soon comprehend!).
    "We must go! Quickly!" said Metoro, "to the hangar.
This wild storm may not let up until morning—
And perhaps not even then. Come, my friends. It is warm;
There's a hot stove and some cots I've prepared inside."
    We did not need any further suggestion. In haste,
Grabbing our gear and the well-padded box that contained
Those sundered shards of "Harappan," the Indus' script,
We moved in haste toward the beckoning hangar's lights
Feeling quite safe—though only a generator
Artificially held off The Dark that first night.

...they appeared—
By the fierce forks of the lightning to seem alive!

* * *

By the next dawning the storm was over and we went
To Metoro's small dwelling less than a mile away.
A humble cottage resting beneath Ranu Kau,
The tall bowl-shaped and now dormant volcano resting
On the southwestern headland of Rapa Nui.

    After our breakfast, he brought out his big find.
It was the blade of an oar, ancient, but still intact.
Upon our examination, we knew beyond doubt
The ancient script of that culture so far away—
As distant in years as in miles from Harappa—
Was a recording of the very same language.
But we were still unsure what that lost tongue was.

    I then unwrapped the two halves of our discovery.
And then Metoro gave out—first a gasp—*then a cry!*

    "What you have here, my good friends, is a wonder!
I have no longer a doubt that this script is the same
That our own 'Talking Wood' depicts. You see!
Both of these two, newly discovered examples
They have in common *at least five new signs*
That neither script showed before! And yet there are two
That I have seen in the markings in our caves:
This one with bat wings—we call them *the 'Gantas'*;
Tales say this other one here is a *'Shaggat.'"*

    He pointed out then the second sign that I had joked,
"Looks like a pizza. I like mine with pepperoni."
We had all laughed—Petrovich, Smith, and I—
At the odd circular symbol surrounding small dots.

    "You would not laugh," said Metoro, "Shaggat very bad.
Both of these signs—very Evil. *Very great horrors*
Are to be seen in the signs in our two texts!

"I am convinced, more than ever, we must think von Junzt
Has sent us the dread lost tongue we must use to compare
Here to both your new text and to my 'Talking Wood.'"
    Then Smith said, "Yes, Metoro, I believe you are right.
We should assume the *Necronomicon*'s vile tongue
That the infamous Al-Hazred translated for us
Is both transcribed in these signs and on your oar blade.
Let us proceed thinking some of these are true word signs—
Like your 'Shaggat' and 'Gantas'—but many are sounds:
That a *syllabary* is also working here.
    Let us then study the frequency of occurrence
Of both your Rongorongo glyphs and our Indus shapes.
And if they index the 'Mad Arab's' language
We'll have our proof that we've solved two lost systems—
Though very wondrous it is that these two should connect!"
    "It would be 'wondrous' yes, but omenous also,"
I added, contemplating just what that might mean.
I put no stock in it. For the texts must be mythic…
Dark superstitions to frighten their folk, to put
'Fear of the gods'—but how shared? How in common?"
    "At the very least, it's no simple inventory.
It's no dull shopping list for the local store."
The Russian said. " We've true literature here!
Also to show seeming disparate tongues are one!
We shall be famous twice over my friends! Rejoice!"

* * *

    It was at noon that same day that we climbed to the top
Of Terevaka, the highest accessible point.
Just as with all of the island's volcanoes,
It had been dormant for centuries. The huge

And pond-bespeckled low basin of Rana Roraku
Far down the slope and below us was beautiful,
But far more awesome the vistas of ocean around us!
   For the whole island could be seen from that vantage point,
And the broad sea spread before us in all directions;
    Indeed it seemed as if we were the Center of Earth!
The nearest land with inhabitants was Pitcairn—
Nearly 2000 kilometers off to the west
With a mere fifty inhabitants—a few
Left with the surname of "Christian," the descendants
Of the old legend of mutiny—*Bounty*'s First Mate.
   A thousand miles to the southwest was "Point Nemo,"
The Latin for "No One" and the farthest from any land
Of any point on our Earth—"Inacessability's Pole."
And one could easily feel from that volcanic crest
The entire world was, indeed, a flat circle, vast—
With the horizon it's Edge and the World's End.
   Then we walked back a good distance to Metoro's home,
Not far from the strange weirding place—Orongo,
Ancient and mystical circular huts. But his
House was away from the sheer, high cliff faces
Down on a gentler mild slope toward the sea it lay.
There we began to peruse the inscriptions
Trying to find if there was correlation
Between our glyphs and the guttural sounds
Of that most heinous language set down by Al-Hazred
Of the dread *Necronomicon* von Junzt had sent.

* * *

   We took one morning to survey more of the wonders
Which that strange island held in the vastness of ocean.

45

Of many thousands of petroglyphs etched in stone,
There were several that bore the same strange symbols
That had been newly discovered on the oar and the shards.
　　And there were also the *Ahu*, odd platforms of stone.
Most, simply raised up, looking out to the ocean, with some
Bearing tall moai, some like raised floors. Daises?
For what odd ceremonies? All lost to Time. And some,
When they were excavated, held ossuaries, yet most
Were rubble-filled. They had ramps on the landward side
Fanned out for access. But accessed for what purposes?

* * *

　　That afternoon we met up with some islanders
They were quite surly and all gave us evil glances.
But friend Metoro was quick to admonish their leader:
"Begone, Ngatavake! You and your clansmen! Go practice
Your insane blasphemies some other place! Your cult
Is a great insult to all of our kinfolk. You
Seek to bring back ways you don't comprehend."

　　　　　　　　　　　　　　　　　　　　The man
Turned to Metoro and spat on the earth. "You say
That I am ignorant of the ways of our Fathers, But I
Say to you and these foreigners here. It is *you*
Who are now tempting a great reawakening!
Even by reading old words, secret chants. Know this!
There are some verses and curses that can be unlocked
　Merely by knowing them, not even speaking out loud!"
　　Once more Metoro in flyting rejoinder, spoke
Out in defiance, against Ngatavake. "Go!
You and your clan are abominations, defiling
Our home, our island—Yes! all Rapa Nui

46

Look down like Moai at your sinful ways. Your clan
With its vile teachings and perverted rites has no power."
    Then it was over, but I sensed in Metoro, unease
As we went back to his homestead, and when I asked
Of this strange man and his cult, he paused briefly. Then:
    "He is a priest, in a way, that foul man Ngatavake.
He and his followers worship strange idols.
But I am troubled by rituals I've watched in hiding,
As his clan meet at Orongo *on nights of no moon*.
    There, on an ahu that looks to the southwest,
Over the steep cliff above the Great Sea, they chant
And they dance all round a black stone idol. And they
Cover their bodies with symbols in black. And some
Of the markings are the same as the glyphs we study!
    Also it troubles me that Ngatavake seems
To be aware of the work that we do on the glyphs.
I don't believe they could know of the texts we translate,
Yet I am bothered. Perhaps some connection exists
Between their rites and the glyphs we research? But I
Cannot believe it is more than coincidence. Yet…"
    So, my misgivings increased. Could this foul text
Actually hold some abhorrent dire truths?

                    * * *

    The next few days we had made some real progress. But we
Were quite appalled by the words now emerging!
Although they certainly must be mere horrific legends,
And were revealing new additions dire to the
Horrific text that Al-Hazred had glossed, we all
Felt a strong sense of unease at the translation's import.
There were incantations, chants, and invocations—

Clearly intended to call up pure Evils. And harsh,
Ugly, and guttural were all the sounds. A more
Vile and cacophonous tongue ne'er existed!

* * *

    Then came the night I shall never be able to
Fully erase from my memories—try as I might.
For we had finally translated the shards; and also
The "Wood that Talks" on the blade of that cursed oar.
Feeling quite ill, I went out to the slope 'neath the stars,
    But—as I looked over high Ranu Kau—I saw…
Over the moonlit volcanic basin there wheeled,
Too large for birds, nine winged shapes in the night. Just then
Metoro too had come out…then he cried: "Ayeee!
They are the *Gantas! Demacrados nocturnos!*
They are *demonios alados de la noche!* I have
Seen them before only in my mind's eye. Nightmares
That I had thought to be only a legend. We must
Pause in our efforts to work with these texts! My friend,
This is dire proof that our work at decipherment
Truly is stirring up echoes of Evil. Also, hear!
There are low chants up the slope at Orongo."
    Quickly Metoro and I climbed up the steep incline
To a high edge of the dormant volcano.
There, by the light of the moon in its fullness,
In the dark lake in the crater of Ranu Kau
There were dark shapes that were surfacing there—
All in a slithering motion! We saw their wakes
Cutting the waters. And far, far above there wheeled
The horrible nine! Great bat-things with shrill chattering!

There were dark shapes that were surfacing there—
All in a slithering motion! We saw their wakes
Cutting the waters. And far, far above there wheeled
The horrible nine! Great bat-things with shrill chattering!

Then, looking down on the huts of Orongo—
That prehistoric cluster of huts—we saw
That weird priest Ngatavake and his minions.
The were all chanting and dancing around a black stone—
Beside it a litter they had used to carry that idol
That was the object of their rites up to the large ahu
Perched on the cliff-face o'erlooking the Deep.
    There, to the southwest, the full moon was wending,
Colored like blood setting low in the black sky.
Like the red eye of a demon it lit up a "pathway"
Along the black sea to the shore of Rapa Nui.
    Then—to our Horror!—the chanters moved forward,
Up to the edge…and then…over the cliff! Each crying
Out in strange words that we could not comprehend
From the great height as we stared in amazement.
The fall was three hundred feet to the rocks of the coast!
That awful group suicide we could not believe,
And we both lay for a moment in silence there.

Then—to our Horror!—the chanters moved forward,
Up to the edge...and then...over the cliff!

But then Metoro said, "Look! There near my homestead,
What is that glowing? There! Under the water?"
    Far down the slope lay Metoro's small cabin
On a far gentler incline heading down to the ocean.
In the dark waters off shore a sub-surface green light,
With a weird pulsating glow and quite huge in girth,
Was moving slowly toward the broad shoreline!
    We could see Smith and Petrovich run down the slope,
Both evidently enthralled by the spectacle.
We also began to rush down to the cabin,
Only arriving as our friends entered the surf.
We then were about to follow after them.
But, suddenly, we halted, stopped dead in our tracks!

* * *

    Darker than night, far more black than the sea's stark jet,
Rose an amorphous, unholy thing I can see yet—
In all my nightmares it floats coming closer to land,
But then it heaved its great bulk up onto the strand!
It was the eyes—yes—the eyes that I'll never forget,
For there were thousands of them! shifting about
Over that blob of black slime. Then—in a terrorized scream:
"Oh! A Shaggat! A Shaggat!" Metoro cried out.
He grabbed my arm, pulled me back. Then we turned and ran.
The very next moment, the terrible screaming began.

* * *

* * *

We dared to return at the first cold, grey light of dawn,
Metoro's home was destroyed; Horace Smith was gone!
But my gorge rose when I saw, lying there—more than dead—
That poor gelatinous thing that was missing its head!
Every bone of the skeleton could be seen through
That horrid translucent thing now turned into goo—
Yet clearly Petrovich, once the man we well knew.
Those grim remains we burned 'neath a moai nearby,
And we watched as the acrid smoke roiled through the sky.

* * *

Before that dread night and the day that had followed,
We had deciphered the shards to the very last word.
"It is mere myth," we had told ourselves—terrible, yes,
But, "It could never be true." Not that tale we had heard
From old Metoro, and read in Abdul Al-Hazred—
In that cursed *Necronomicon*. The spurious *Scroll of the Dead*
Could not be real!—true accounts of this world! Yet clearly
Those final syllables had to be uttered: "Fa-Ta-Gun."
Little we knew what our solving that text had begun.
Before I departed next day from Rapa Nui,
There were no bodies to be found on the rocks
Below the high cliff-face at Orongo. The Sea—
Or far more likely some horrendous, dark Evil—
Finally claimed Ngatavake and all his foul clan.
I stood among the moai, looking out to the West.
But, when the sun's blood-red disk sank toward the sea,
In abject fear I turned 'round and I hastily fled
Back to the air strip where Metoro sought to calm me,
Although I knew I'd be plagued where'er my path led.

I would be moving to Arkham to join von Junzt.
Where I would learn that young Dexter had gone
Quite insane while at reading in Al-Hazred's tome
And then had taken his own life with a dagger of bone!
    Yet we'd continue to study the text more minutely. Von Junzt
And I in Miskatonic's deep nethermost vaults.

* * *

                                        But now
The great discovery must be suppressed. No one—
Except for Metoro, von Junzt, and myself—can know
Of the Horrors contained in that text. The missing
Lines from *that Book* that Al-Hazred had scanned. The chants
That can awaken the curse of the Cosmos! No!
We had to be sure that those words are not uttered, be
Wary in even the study of that eldritch tongue.
    With mixed emotions I boarded the plane that morning
For Santiago and thence to the States. I waved
To brave Metoro and attempted a smile. Who knew
What dreadful challenges might lie there before him?
As the plane banked for its turn to the east, I looked
Out at the sea beyond Ranu Kau, seemingly endless,
Glistening bright in the morning sun's rays. But I knew
Now what dread secrets lay deep 'neath those waters. I
Found myself shuddering—knowing what lies beneath!

* * *

    After von Junzt and I finished the ciphering,
There in old Arkham at Miskatonic,
After we realized the Horrors contained therein,
Into a crucible fired hot as Hell, we placed

Both of the shards and Metoro's oar blade. And then,
After we ground all the remnants to dust, we burnt
All of our manuscripts, notes on that most damnable,
And most accursed foul language that humankind
Ever devised. Yet we cannot erase from mind,
That eldritch knowledge of Cosmic Oblivion!
Held in those words that must die with our deaths!
Never go seeking to repeat our researches.
Pray you beware the Indus and Rapa Nui scripts.
Know that, in following those trails of Evil, The
Ultimate outcome is a fate graver than Death....
Not only for you—but our world as a whole! There are,
From the Deep Cosmos, vile eldritch entities—
That long ago were expelled but they threaten
A dread return—nay! a reawakening!

EPILOGUE

For some dire reason I've felt a compulsion to
Set down this story and now I have answered.
Thus, I will end my strange tale I should never have writ.
*   Though far remote, from all other shores is Easter Island,*
A thousand miles to its southwest Point Nemo sits over
What the Harappan syllables scan as Re-Lay-Ah.
There, 'neath the point farthest from any land mass,
In those black deeps, we must pray that Forever
(What few folk know—and what most could not understand)
That horrid Sleeper, though Dead!, Ka-Thu-Lu lies Dreaming there.

Frank Coffman

NOTES

ON COMPOSITION: In my long poem above, I have only approximated this meter, and there are many variant lines. I have also considered a system of unstressed syllable, moderate stressed syllable, and dominant stressed syllable with the usual system of 1, 2, 3 for the scansion mode of u, \, and / respectively. Furthermore, I have considered moderate stresses to count as unstressed syllables, seeking to have this "rising meter," ideally, to have the major accents in the 4th, 7th, 10th, and 12th syllable positions. This has not always been possible—over such a lengthy text.

[1] DRUTAVILAMBITA (a 12 syllable podic meter—i.e. measured in metrical feet)
- The word means "scan quick and slow."
- The metre Drutavilambita consists of twelve syllables.
- In this meter, the 4th, the 7th, the 10th and the 12th syllables are long—or in the case of an English approximation—stressed/accented: uuu/uu/uu/u/
- Thus, in English, the meter is approximated by one 4th Paeon, two Anapests, and one Iamb.
- The metre is termed as Drutavilambita for the varying notes of intonations because we find *talas* (like metrical "feet") of varying denomination: i.e. *druta* and *vilambita* in a musical note.
- Critical Comment: It is to be noted that in the domain of Sanskrit Prosody this meter enjoys considerable amount of popularity.
- The celebrated poet, Deokota used this metre in his *Sulochana Kavya*.

[2] BISCRIPT: Is a parallel passage of text showing the written characters of two different writing systems. The most famous of these is the Rosetta Stone (actually a "triscript" since both Hieratic and Hieroglyphic characters exist alongside the Greek) that became the key to Champollion's initial decipherment steps in unlocking the alphabetic system and glyphs of Ancient Egyptian.

[3] INDO-IRANIAN—one of the major sub-families of INDO-EUROPEAN (q.v.)

[4] PROTO-INDO-EUROPEAN (or P.I.E. as most linguists call it) is the reconstructed parent language of almost all of the various languages of Europe, India, and Persia. It also includes ancient Hittite.

[5] GÖBEKLI TEPE—a site discovered in the extreme South of Turkey where excavations have uncovered many circles of standing stones, featuring tall monoliths decorated with elaborate carvings of animals and various other shapes. It has been dated to be at least 13,000 years old! The site has turned former beliefs about the abilities of "hunter-gatherer" prehistoric societies on their heads.

57

[6] BOUSTROPHEDON—Literally from the Greek: "like the turn of the ox" (in plowing rows.) Curiously, several ancient scripts used a back-and-forth method of writing—going from left to right in one line and right to left in the next (or vice versa); sometimes even the glyphs or signs were reversed in orientation in this method. Sometimes each succeeding line was written (in effect) in the same direction, BUT the medium turned or reversed so that it read in the opposite direction (see REVERSE BOUSTROPHEDON below).

WRITING SYSTEMS: The first four are the most frequent systems of writing that have been developed.

A ALPHABETIC (the word deriving, of course, from the Greek first two letters: alpha and beta) systems use signs to represent single sounds or at least various phonemes that can be represented by that sound (i.e. vowels such as "A" that can be "long," "short," "schwa," etc.). There are usually between 18 (as in Hawaiian) and 33 or so (as in Russian) signs used in such a system – occasionally more.

B A SYLLABARY, such as that used in Sumerian Cuneiform (later used by many languages) usually has from 80 to 120 signs, each representing a syllable (usually consonant plus vowel as with "ba, be, bi, bo, bu," but sometimes the reverse as with "am, em, im, om, um," and rarely consonants around vowels as with "mat" and, even more rare, single vowels.

C A LOGOGRAPH is, as the Greek of the word says: "Word Picture."
The Chinese system of over 10,000 symbols is close to this, yet each of those thousands of symbols must, in different contexts, mean several different things—since there are more than 10,000 thoughts in any human imagination. Chapman in the story, assumes that the Indus script, with its approximately 400 signs, is, most likely, *D* LOGO-SYLLABIC with some signs as "word signs" or LOGOGRAMS but most as a SYLLABARY. Ancient Egyptian Hieroglyphics proved to be quite amazing in that it is a blend of alphabetic, syllabic, and ideographic—with the added complication that, often, a sign-symbol for a whole word or idea is then ALSO alphabeto-syllabically "spelled out" beside the sign in an intentional redundancy—thus, of course, adding to the mystery, the secrecy, and the beauty of their inscriptions and paintings.

E A REBUS is usually a combination of a homonymic picture and an letter—for example, a picture of an APE followed by the letter X for "apex."

An *F* IDEOGRAM is, pretty much the same as a LOGOGRAM except that the former has more of the sense of idea signified by the word and the latter

58

more of the sense of the word that indexes the idea or thought. For all practical purposes, they are synonymous.

⁷ PROTO-DRAVIDIAN is a reconstructed sub-family of INDO-IRANI-AN (q.v.). The language was spoken by the ancestors of modern Dravidian Indians who live mostly in the South of the country.

⁸ In Egyptian hieroglyphics, the ideograms/logograms that signify a whole word or concept or idea are DETERMINANTS of meaning, usually accompanied by alphabetic and syllabic signs that reiterate the word phonetically in addition to the symbolism of the determinant. Sometimes these have a grammatical function as the triplication of a sign or mark to signify plurality.

⁹ KV55—"Valley of the Kings, Tomb Number 55" This tomb is believed by many to have contained the mummy of the disgraced pharaoh, Akhenaten, whose reign saw the abandonment of the old gods in favor of a the monotheistic worship of "the Aten"—the disk of the sun, the giver of all life. Although DNA analysis has shown that the mummy found therein is, indeed, the son of Amenhotep III and the father of Tutankhamun ["Tut"]—which would clearly indicate Akhenaten—some have disputed these findings. But consistent with the defacing of most images of Akhenaten and also of his sister-wife Nefertiti, the arrangement of the tomb (canopic jars and ushabti figures facing the wrong way, as if to keep the soul trapped within the tomb and not, as normal, encouraging it to "go forth by day" [*pert em hru* in Ancient Egyptian] and be free. Furthermore, a curse was found inscribed on the wall of the stairway going down the short distance to the tomb chamber: "The Evil One shall not live again." This would be in keeping with the wishes of the priests of the old pantheon to destroy both Akhenaten's memory and his attempt at imposed monotheism.

¹⁰ REVERSE BOUSTROPHEDON—is a system in which the text in alternate lines is rotated 180 degrees rather than mirrored.

SONNETS FOR THE DEAD OF NIGHT

Frank Coffman

I
A Short Tale Retold
[after Poe]

(a Coffman Sonnet, Type 2V)

I loved the old man, but he had to die!
He'd never done me wrong, I must admit.
I think it was his eye. Yes, that was it.
I loathed the sight of that pale, evil eye.

Filmed over, with a cast of sickly blue,
It haunted my nightmares each night until
I knew I had to end it with his death.
I smothered him with bedding, 'til I knew—
As he quit struggling and he lay quite still—
That he had breathed his last abhorrent breath.

I quickly dismembered him—a grisly chore!
I hid it 'neath the floorboards of his room.
I knew no one would ever find his tomb.
Wait! There's a knock. Oh! Someone's at the door!

II
The Line
(a Coffman Sonnet, Type 5E*)

Somewhere there's a line, if penned, all would be beguiled!
It would chill all hearts and all souls terrify.
Dark poets have sought it in the deeps of sky,
In winds that whip the willow rushes wild,
In black pools where the waters never lie
Quite restless, in stark images beviled,
In words of horror upon horror piled!

But rare and few those poets who came nigh
To crafting such a line with weirding art.
Poe sought to find that powerful verse accursed.
And Lovecraft strove such horror to impart.
Full many since believed it could be versed.

Perhaps it's best that line should never be.
Who knows what—through its chant—might be set free?

III
A Haunting
(a Rhymed Fibonacci Sonnet)

Grim,
Gaunt,
Ghastly,
Glistening
Vision of a ghost
Appears before his startled eyes.
Then, behind it, a multitude of phantoms appears,
Approaches him, arousing heretofore unknown fears.
"They cannot be!" his reason cries.
Meanwhile the vast host,
Listening,
Lastly
Haunt
Him.

IV
He Who Waits
(an Italian Sonnet)

I am the Watcher, and I stand in wait,
As long as Life has lasted on this Earth.
The hells of human tragedy, the heights of mirth,
The deeper happinesses, and the depths of hate,
All, all I've seen—the ends of Chance and Fate,
The years that bounty and the years that dearth
Have spun around this old Orb since its birth.
I've watched and waited here beside *The Gate.*

Oh yes, I have been waiting all these years,
Was ancient when Atlantis met it's doom,
Watched Babel's Tower and great Pyramids grow.
I know the range of mankind's hopes and fears
And know the thing most fear most is the tomb.
I wait. *Et in Arcadia Ego.*

Frank Coffman

V
Beyond The Veil
(an Envelope Sonnet:
Octave of two Italian Quatrains but differently rhymed)

Some few have journeyed out beyond *The Veil*.
Of those that venture, fewer still come back.
Dark tomes hold hidden spells to look, but lack
The black, archaic words that will not fail
To bring the seeker home to this our realm.
From this side, only shadowy shapes uncertain
Beckon and stir behind that tenebrous curtain—
And what waits there would quickly overwhelm.

Best not to look—but much worse that way to travel,
For its secrets are kept from no living soul forever;
There is time enough to wait for the Hand of Fate.
And those who return are changed. Their minds unravel;
Their rantings hold one theme: a wish they had never
Traversed a path so cursed…but now—too late!

VI
The Old Ones
(a Ghazal Sonnet, invented form*)

In darkest cosmic deeps there dwell The Old Ones.
Far worse than devils from our nearer Hell, The Old Ones.

They plan to come again from the Abyss
To rule—as dreadful tales foretell—The Old Ones!

It numbs the mind to know they have begun!
They scheme to ring out Mankind's knell—The Old Ones.

Once, long ages ago, we found a way
To oust these terrors. Yes! To expel The Old Ones.

Now, yet again, their Darkness shrouds our day,
With Evils we've forgotten how to quell. The Old Ones

Infest the blackest corners of our lore
With heinous horrors that know no parallel—The Old Ones!

Oh no! They're coming—as they came before—
With us to dwell. And no soul can repel The Old Ones!

VII
Roundmoon Ritual
(a Brisbane Sonnet)

Sure as our old moon shows his fabled face,
Quite at the full (whether at perigee
Or apogee or some zone in between)
Those victims who are of that curséd race—
The lycanthropes—are forced to forage free.
If you are fortunate…never to be seen!

For, like the tides, the night orb's ebb and flood
Mark out scant weeks of normal calm or strife,
Until the next round disk comes 'round again
To signal a new waxing tide of blood,
Another horrid harvest of human life,
Gleaned ghastly by wolven wights once normal men.

And so, the Cycles of the Moon roll on.
When Luna gorges, some won't see the dawn.

VIII
Indelible Vision
(an English Sonnet)

The others made me do it on a dare.
There were five of us, carousing late one night.
John noticed the old cemetery there,
Close by the forest, clear in a full moon's light.
   I was the newest member of that gang
Of college chums. We'd had our fill of beer.
Not wishing to endure the quartet's harangue,
I walked right in. Though felt—I *showed* no fear.
   "It's just one restless night," was in my mind.
The graveyard air was chill, mists lingering
About the stones.
              When something—undefined
At first—drew closer....Then I beheld *The Thing!*

A bloody, floating, scarlet skull that screams
Has burned into my soul—haunts all my dreams!

IX
Legend of the Lich
(a Terza Rima Sonnet*)

Using fowl, fell grimoires and lore most eldritch,
His soul was compressed into a void-black jewel.
Thus he transformed—fell Sorcerer to Lich.

Immortal—he thought—planned he Night's Realm to rule.
All forms of wicked wights he sent abroad;
He raised the Dead with Necromancies cruel.

All Things most cursed, anathema to God,
He loosed upon the land. A thick, miasmic mist
Roiled o'er that region, laid thousands under sod.

He then sought Satan's vile aid to enlist—
That Wizard most wicked with a separable soul.
But for the Devil's Mill his black-jewel soul was grist.

Not reckoning such a bargain had its toll!
The Lich is gone. O'er now barren lands the long years roll.

X
Night Shapes

(a Brisbane Sonnet)

Especially where umbrageous shadows deep
Bedarken wild and wooded regions drear,
One may glimpse them flit past the "corner of the eye."
Amorphous like shades in nightmare-haunted sleep,
They rouse in us the essence of stark fear—
The *Rex Terrorem*—when we deem such things are nigh.

But "Of course," our Reason argues, "These shifting shapes
Cannot be real creatures that could harm;
They're mere delusions, optical illusions…."
But They are there!—and Reason quite escapes
When we chance to look full at them. Our alarm
Is justified. Yes! They often make intrusions
Into our zone. And those cursed plainly see
The Nyctomorphs are here!–near you and me.

Frank Coffman

XI
Point of View
(an English Sonnet)

This place is haunted. As I know in deepest woe,
For I am bound unto a horrid fate.
I've gone where living souls can never go,
But for an unwise few—who learned too late.

I thought that I'd be happy as his wife,
But he was a monster from the very start.
One day, he killed me with his hunting knife—
I ran, but cornered, he calmly pierced my heart!
That scene replays! I run, I'm stabbed, I fall....
He wrapped me in canvas soaked with lye and oil.
My once fair form now rots behind this wall.
No sign was left, so careful was his toil.
    Now I reprise my murder—until some friend
    Might see my haunting truth, my curse to end.

XII
Re-Creation

(a Brisbane Sonnet)

"Did I request Thee, Maker, from my clay
To mold me man? Did I solicit thee
From Darkness to promote me...."
—Milton, *Paradise Lost*

Galvani's experiments had shown the way:
Electro-chemical reactions clear!
That frog leg spasm kicked Victor's mind alive
With a grand design from which he could not sway.
Found out, he'd be condemned—but he did not fear.
The dead could return to life—and even thrive!

His secret work went on; his papers shocking
His peers: "Such powers are reserved for God!"
"It's morally repugnant even to explore!"
Yet, despite all scorn, despite disgrace and mocking,
The young doctor pressed on with steady plod—
Until, one stormy night, *The Veil* he tore!

His assembled man awoke and twitched to life.
He hadn't expected the *Thing* would want a wife!

Frank Coffman

XIII
The Skald Sings of Samhain

(a sonnet primarily in the Old Norse form of Dróttkvaett*—
with some lines in Hyrnhent* and some in Draughent*)

All Hallows' Eve. Hurry, harry the still-living,
Fell foes with Hell's fury, freely roaming, laughing,
As mortal Man, failing, most feebly to resist
Potent attacks prevailing. Powers they might enlist
Are oft too long delayed. The Might of great Mages,
Some strong enough, indeed, schooled from the secret pages
Of grand grimoires, able, through lost incantations
When the World is unstable, to win o'er Mis-creations.

Terrors, the Veil tearing, travel in our demesne.
Hostile the Host bearing Horrors of Halloween.
Legion of Evil laughing, at the Lost who disbelieve.
Most mortals keep scoffing; for many—no reprieve.
Wicked wights all wending—when that *Great Gossamer* tatters—
Into Our World, sending such Things our sanity shatters.

73

XIV
Georgics for Cthulhu
(a sonnet in Hexameters*)

Deep! far beneath the Pacific, lies the dark region of R'lyeh.
Strange is the glow of that city! Green, it makes sinister shadows
There 'mongst the inky obsidian structures, indistinct in that twilight.
Stranger the farmers and husbanders, forms pseudo-manlike—and morphing!
Theirs the great duty to tend to spawn of the City's detritus:
Some are ophidian, sinuous, slithering horrors; others cephalopod,
Mimicking poorly their Master who sleeps in the City's dark center.
And there are strange underwater Bat-things with weird scaly wings
Flitting about there—gloom shrouded terrible flyers, fleet in the blackness.
Meanwhile the tenders must nurture carnivorous plants in R'lyeh's gardens,
Watch 'oer those waving weeds, poisoning all of those currents of Chaos.
Blooms that ooze blood are abundant; all must be carefully tended.
Ranchers who herd nothing of Reason; farmers who grow naught but Fear,
Tending where Cthulhu lies sleeping—dreaming although he is Dead!

XV
Nachzehrer*
(a Minnesang Sonnet Sequence*)
based upon the Middle High German form)

1

If one meets death by one's own hand,
Or, rarely, after accident,**
Or first to die from a plague's curse,
A horrid *Nachzehrer* may rise.

This fiend awakes and roams the land,
Feeds on the dead—its foul intent.
But first it stalks and brings—much worse—
Its own kinfolk to their demise.

So ravenous it's said they be,
Some of their own flesh with great glee
These Things devour! They can shapeshift
And take the form of any beast.
Kith, acquaintances have short shrift
Before these Horrors have their feast.

2

First the dread Thing devours its shroud,
But then gorges *on its own flesh!*
Meanwhile, survivors in its clan
Sicken and die, but then comes worse!

It's said its eating is most loud
When new in grave, body still fresh,

Disgusting sounds of eating can
Be heard above that place accursed.

And soon, by night, the fiend crawls out,
Begins its roaming all about.
First, it will seek a near church tower
And ring its bell. Then all who hear
Are doomed by that sound's dreaded power.
They will be dead within the year.

3
And then this spawn of Hell *seeks out
Its fated family and friends!*—
Kills and devours them, some abed,
Some, despite safeguards, overcome.

Their flesh is rent, and gory gouts
Bedeck scenes where they meet their ends.
Full soon that dire *Thing's* clan is dead—
Torn asunder, they met their doom.

Once sated, it returns to ground,
But, if by day, perchance it's found
There is a way for it to die—
A second, final death to deal.
But first, one must identify
This horrid wight to know it's real:

4
Uncovered, open the casket lid.
If its left thumb is in right fist,
And open wide left eye alone,
Gaunt, naked—flesh morsels missing, gone!

'Tis proof a Nachzehrer was hid.
Then you must these things enlist:
A well-honed sword, a coin, a stone.
To end the *Thing* you gaze upon.

First, open wide that gory maw;
Force coin and stone into that jaw.
Then, deftly take the sharpened blade
And quick behead that demon beast.
Thus will the foul thing be unmade,
No more to gorge in awful feast.

*The Nachzehrer is a vampire-like revenant, but one not seeking blood, but, rather, human flesh. Found in the lore of especially northern Germany and in Poland. Its attack was not communicable—as a vampire's bite might be.

**Usually, if "by accident," it would be a drowning that would lead to transformation to a Nachzehrer.

XVI
Sad Steps Beneath the Silent Moon

(a Wyatt's Sonnet with variant sestet)

*"With how sad steps, O Moon, thou climb'st the skies.
How silently, and with how wan a face…"*
—Sir Philip Sidney, from *Astrophil & Stella* 31

Those nights the silent moon in fullness slips
Just past, or scuds along the flying clouds,
Or grimly dimmed when welkin dark enshrouds,
Through Summer's haze or when cold Winter grips—
All seasons through the Earth's elliptical trips—
Whether through Autumn's spare branches, or when crowds
Of Springtime foliage dim the moon's stark floods—
An Evil lurks abroad with slavering lips.

Those are the nights the cursed ones change their skins!
And prey upon the rest of humankind.
A bite survived means a horrid life begins
When next the round moon shines. A shape defined
Against that bright orb, cresting on the hill—
A ghastly man-wolf stalking its next kill.

Frank Coffman

XVII
The Socratic Method

(a Brisbane Sonnet)

He'd owned the house for only a few weeks,
Surprised by both the low price and the fact
It had lain vacant for a score of years.
But then—weird noises! then a voice that speaks
Without a sound! kept prompting him to act.
And phantom visions stoked the fires of fears.

The noiseless voice, demonic sights increased
With each day passed within those horrid halls.
It wasn't long before he planned the deed.
His only thought—to have his soul released!
Then putrid panoramas stank the walls—
And then—much worse!—*the walls began to bleed!*

His mind was soon quite gone….He drank the lye.
Escaping! by that horrid way to die.

XVIII
Halloween 2020

(an English Sonnet)

He dreaded it. This month for a second time—
Ironic it should fall on Halloween!—
The rare "Blue Moon" would sail the sky, sublime,
Shine down upon this Earth. Again he'd glean
The horrid harvest. But he'd not be alone!
For others: cursed and damned, demon and ghost,
Vampire and ghoul, all Evils would fill this zone—
And legions of the living would be lost!
Secluded in dens, deep woods, and shuttered homes,
The rites of human sacrifice will endure.
He will not be alone as forth he roams—
Once bitten, twice accursed! There was no cure.
  So, once again this month, he'll change and prowl;
  Once more the wind will carry a werewolf's howl.

Frank Coffman

XIX
Lawrence Talbot

(an English Sonnet—with a nod,
and perhaps, an apology to E. A. Robinson)

Whenever Lawrence Talbot went to town,
The locals in the quaint shops looked at him.
He was a gentleman from sole to crown,
Well-favored (though sometimes his look was grim).
And he was always splendidly arrayed,
And he was always "*human*" when he spoke.
But Lawrence held a secret, was dismayed
Each monthnight when the frowning round moon broke
Through clouds or glared down from the clear, cold sky.
Those times, you see, Lawrence was "not quite right."
And someone in the drear of dark would die!
For, as a wolf-thing, Lawrence prowled the night.

Until, that night, a silver-handled cane
Crushed down upon his skull—a werewolf's bane.

XX
Old Words
(a Brisbane Sonnet
—in theoretical Proto-World* grammar—
as applied to English)

That forest Earth's center at great danger poses
Though bright flowers its dark trees around grow.
Its black depths within dire, terrible threat dwells.
Horrible danger that wood's depths inside encloses;
No one its ensorcelled secrets of should know.
The ancient Legend an ominous threat foretells.

None who The Grimwood nearby live in dares to go—
But a few who sad mischance through it into have wandered.
Those doomed souls its depths from out never come.
Weird, greenish lights the night through it in glow.
Ghostly voices the Lost of that forest from are heard.
Screaming Souls the wind on that Wild in aimlessly roam.

Stranger, who that Weirdwood near chance by travels,
Thy Soul oblivion nears; sheer Horror in a Mind unravels.

XXI
Split Person-alities:
Two "Double Exposure" Sonnets

1. (an Interlocking Rubáiyát Sonnet)

On most days of each month, on most every night—
Except when Earth lies under the full moon's light—
No one would see the Beast beneath his skin;
No one would guess the horror of his plight;
None know sheer Terror to see that slavering grin—
None would suspect the lupine lust within,
Revealed all months beneath the Moon's round Face.
And yet—he's guilty of the greatest Sin.
Foul Murder, eldest crime of our sinful race.
Those nights, the features of a wolf replace
A Man's fine form and truly handsome visage—
Whatever had been Good. Now transformed to the Base—
Becomes a Creature hunting with bloody rage.
The werewolf of folk tale and mythic page.

2. (an Italian Sonnet)

Within us all lie two innate extremes.
Between our Darker Angels and the Bright,
Between the bright Day's noon and darkest Night,
Between the stuff of Nightmares and of Dreams,
We—most of us—live our little lives it seems
Along the spectrum between Wrong and Right,
With one or the other winning this Inner Fight,
Displaying every hue of Life's Light's split Beams.

But there was one who fought the Evil Twin;
    One brilliant doctor formed a dangerous plan;
There was a way, he thought, the Good could win;
    The Evil could be banished from a man!
But Henry Jekyll delved too deep within.
    Alas! The horror of Mr. Hyde began.

XXII
The Algul

(a sonnet in transposed Arabic Tawīl [Long] Meter*)

Among the most horrid Djinns, the Algul in woman's form,
By night is in quest for blood from either the Living or Dead.
Especially blood from children craved by this horrid ghoul,
Vampiric, insatiable—a *Thing* that fills all with dread.
It lures into dark, secluded places the unwary young,
And there, in the gory gloom, they are of life's essence bled.
Sometimes it will enter homes. And sleeping small children kill,
By taking their breath away and draining 'til life has fled.

More horrid its thirst when living souls can't be found to take,
It roams through the boneyards, digging deep into children's graves.
And sucks out remaining blood from bodies! Defilement macabre.
The graveyard its home, but wanders wide—questing what it craves.
Some say they're the spawn of Lillith, Queen of the Evil Realms.
Vampiric Alguls. Some pray, some chant, but it's only Chance that saves.

XXIII
Close Behind

(a Coffman Sonnet, Type 2V*)

"Like one, that on a lonesome road
Doth walk in fear and dread,
And having once turned round walks on,
And turns no more his head;
Because he knows, a frightful fiend
Doth close behind him tread."

—Coleridge,
"The Rime of the Ancient Mariner"

Those flitting forms you think you sometimes see,
Shadows through fog or mist in strange shapes, seeming
To defy all reason—though they appear to be
Close to mankind in mold, like things in dreaming—
Or rather glimpsed in Nightmares—*Exist! You are awake!*
The movement fleeting past "the corner of the eye"
That made you turn and stare—yet nothing's there!—
Should not be simply dismissed. For your soul's sake,
Know that these *Things* have been with Us for aye.
Learn that there are good reasons to beware!

Whether *They* are "close behind," just out of sight
Beside you, peripheral, just beyond clear vision's ken,
They are the spawn of the darkest kind of Night,
Long banished—*They* are coming forth again!

Frank Coffman

XXIV
The Bunyip
(in Australian/Bowlesian Sonnets)

1.
A warning to all who plan to go "Down Under":
Take heed to this—I swear its true!—short rhyme.
Know that there dwells in Australia's sunny clime
A monstrous beast, a most unnatural wonder!

It's called by many names in many a tongue.
For more than two hundred languages were spoken
By indigenous folk 'ere that continent was broken
By new settlers to that ancient land from dim past sprung.

Aboriginal tales from 'round that giant isle
Tell of a thing that dwells in ponds and lakes,
In rivers and billabongs. Its thirst it slakes
With blood! But it's no giant crocodile.

Though, in the North, huge salt-water reptiles thrive,
This thing is a bane to all who walk alive.

2.
Yes, the dread Bunyip lives in the land of "Oz."
And those who would any water wander near
Will often feel a rush of sudden fear
They can't explain—but then they feel its jaws!

Curiously, when attempts are made to describe
This horror from the swamps and lakes and pools,
The pictures range across many and various schools
Of thought—differing widely from tribe to tribe.

Perhaps this thing of terror can shift its shape?
Which might explain: "A large dog or a seal,
But with huge tusks!" "No! a clear look will reveal
A long-necked horse or emu with jaws agape!"
"No, it's a giant starfish!" "…has only one eye!
But, if that eye sees you, you are sure to die!"

3.
Of this be sure: by pond's edge or river bank,
Or near a billabong—especially at night—
You risk a meeting with a Thing of Fright!
If you escape, you've Luck or God to thank.

Yes, wild Australia has some curious creatures:
Wombats and platypi, wallabies and 'roos,
Koalas, echidnas—things most see in zoos.
Maybe Taz Tigers? Some claim to have seen its features.

But, strangest of all, this legendary beast
Lurks in its lore, and many think beyond!
Those who wander too close to lake or pond
Just might become the Bunyip's grisly feast.
    Don't think those old, old stories can't be true;
    The next meal of the Bunyip might be YOU!

Frank Coffman

XXV
The Valdemar Effect

(an English Sonnet)

He'd been intrigued by one grim tale by Poe
About a mesmerist and the physical effect—
If one sought the craft of hypnotism to know
And put those skills to use—one could direct
A subject so enthralled to imitate
Symptoms of dread diseases—even Death!

But when he realized it was too late;
The pallor and chill of flesh—yes! But the breath
Had ceased now fully fifteen minutes since,
And ten attempts to end the spell had failed,
He fled that abandoned house and hurried thence,
Back to his flat—dreading what he'd unveiled.

They found him one month later in his bed,
Strangled by hands that dropped flesh one month dead.

XXVI
Long Hidden
(a Decima Italiana* transformed into a Sonnet:
thus, a *Quattordici Italiana**)

There are two graves near north of Rome,
Ages untended those long laid.
Any strangers who that way come
Find nothing but a strange round glade
Surrounded by a forest's gloom.

No markers show above that sward,
There where the centurion fell,
Attempting his fair love to guard
From something from the depths of Hell.
That night they both would meet foul doom.

The local folk do not go near
That weird place where horrors still loom,
Knowing their legend, fraught with fear;
Though—in two patches—spring flowers bloom.

XXVII
Malum ex Machina

(an Coffman Sonnet, Type 2E* followed by a Brisbane Sonnet)

1

As far as paranormal science went,
He was the foremost theorist in the land.
From early days in college he had spent
Now forty years, seeking to understand
Those things that lie beyond most human ken:
Clairvoyance, telekinesis, remote viewing,
Spirits from Beyond—demonic and ghostly—
Satanic rites, ectoplasm, Shadow Men....

Of late, his interest in EVPs renewing,
He'd improved upon the proven devices—mostly
Derived from original "tech"—*but clearer,*
With more immediate feedback of "The Voice."
It seemed to draw the phenomenon's source nearer
And also force them closer with no choice!

2

Indeed, it seemed the device could actually summon
Entities from that *Other Realm* than ours.
And more, much more than single words and phrases,
Full, clearly spoken sentences were common,
And he began to wonder just what powers
The apparatus held. He worked in phases:
First he would merely document conversations
He'd held with *Them.* He kept a neat notebook.

Next, keen curiosity made him query
About their region. And he felt elation
When next *They*—through video channels—let him look!
Though their words thrilled, those visions made him wary!

Too late he realized he'd created a portal
For Horrors—both terrible—and immortal!

Frank Coffman

XXVIII
Ouija

(a Brisbane Sonnet)

The mystic planchette roves 'round to and fro
Among the numerals and letters strewn
About this board of fame and—mayhap?—Fate?
Between the sunface "YES" and moonman "NO.
But are the players at this game immune
From Evils that might find them—soon or late?

Some say, "It's just a pastime, a joke, a toy."
But I contend it opens doorways dire,
Portals that none should pass while yet alive.
And some have died! Or lost all hope of joy
That might have been. Some gazed upon *The Fire
None Hope to See!* In horrid truth—*They* thrive!

Demonic wights at night and noonday dwell
Too close beside us—*and are come from Hell!*

XXIX
The Baba Yaga
(a Russian Dolnik* Sonnet, irregular rhyme)

(In Russian folklore, Baba Yaga flies around in a mortar, wielding a pestle as a weapon. She is a witch [the name translates something like: "crone" or "horror"] who dwells deep in the forest in a strange hut usually described as standing on chicken legs. Though usually malevolent, she may also bestow boons upon those she meets. She has variously been described as either a child-eating monster, or a witch, in commune with forest wildlife, who may be a benefactor.)

In a house upraised on the legs—
Those weird stilts—of a chicken, huge,
The odd witch of the woods there dwells!
If you see her there's no refuge!
Whether good or ill, she casts spells—
That old "Grandmother Horror" weird
When she goes through the trees she floats!
'Tis a tale Russian children have feared
Through long years. Yet—to one who begs—
Blessings can come. Indeed, a boon
May be granted, avoiding grim cells
In that chicken-hut 'neath forest moon.
But with pestle she strikes—and gloats
From her mortar.... Some will die soon.

Frank Coffman

XXX
The Darkroom
(an English Sonnet, followed by a Brisbane Sonnet)

He'd specialized in capturing real estate;
He'd done some architectural odd work.
Seized through his lens, cottage or mansion great
Would show its "best side." But there sometimes lurk—
Since photos catch much more than does the eye
(The human orb must focus near or far.
But, shot at f16, one can descry
Clarity both near and background things that are
Not caught by our vision, limited in range)—
Weird things and oddities. Some negatives will show
Shapes that appear, at first, to be most strange,
Which the positive image proves are things we know.
    Yet this?—a negative of that upstairs space,
    White painted, window-lit, seen now as a reversed place....

Mostly black—save for the varying shades of grey
That marked the portrait on the wall, one pulled-back drape,
The desk by the window...most things as the norm.
Yet there was...something? Just what he could not say.
There seemed a cloud, a wisp...and a round, weird shape
In the far corner...an odd and hoary form?
"Well, this shot's flawed"—aloud. "I'm glad I took
At least three more"—the words now in his head—
"A developing mistake? A queer lens flare?"
But—when the positive emerged—his body shook!
A faint mist was caught mid-swirl. But a face!—quite dead!—
Grinned, jaws agape, with a demonic stare!
    And then, dim lit in red in the darkroom's gloom...
    The Thing was there! And positive as his doom!

XXXI
Yurei
(a Renga Sonnet*:
alternating 17 and 14 syllable lines)

ghosts of restless dead seeking peace in afterlife, purgatory-locked.
whether by cruel murder, unavenged heinous crimes,
seething long-kept hate, perhaps their sad suicide, ceaseless deep sorrow,
lack of proper rites of death—whatever cause, they are trapped!
faint souls cannot leave purgatory's dark limbo, chained between two worlds.
dim spirits lingering until—some resolution be found,
funeral performed, true atonement somehow made, foul crime brought to light.
these *reikon*, spirits of dead, these can be dangerous.
encountering one, you see long, disheveled hair, frightening black strands.
pray that you don't meet its eyes—don't stare at that raised white face!
they envy us here, alive in world lost to them. since forward is blocked,
they often come back to us, arms dangling, gowned all in white,
some floating—no legs!—drifting in aura of flame!—they can bring your death!
yearning for other sad souls, they would have us join them there.

XXXII
The Truly Lost Tribe
(sonnet in Persian Muzari Meter*)

King Nimrod, high and mighty, a great tower did erect.
This haughty grasp for glory, though bold, he did not suspect
God's Anger that would follow this crazed, brazen arrogance.
Once built, that tower sinful was marked, cursed—and it would chance
They who had worked to build it were struck! Mightily confused,
They—who had known one language—now kenned not what others used!
Thus, tribes of many nations went forth, scattered near and far;
Each tribe was isolated and foreign folk squawked: "Bar bar"[1]

Some say that Nimrod, archer—a great hunter as well as king—
Sent arrows from that towertop. Toward Heaven they did sing!
God's Ire was great! To blaspheme! To e'en dare assault the Sky!
King Nimrod, was accursed—yes, but one tribe also to Die!
One group of all those scattered were doomed—damned to Special Hell!
They chant:...*Cthulhu R'lyeh wgah'nagl fhtagn!* Their voices swell.

[1] The word "barbarian" comes from the ancient Greek mimicking of foreign tongues by saying the people sounded like they were saying: "bar bar."

XXXIII
Dyn Blaidd*
(a Sonetti Rispetto*: Types 1 [expanded] and Type 2)

There is a valley in the North of Wales
That holds a deep, dark wood and darker lake.
All those who live near, when the evening fails,
Head homeward by the shortest path to take.
Their children learn the old, old chilling tales
That often make them startle and awake
And listen as the whirling night wind wails
And huddle 'neath their covers 'til daybreak.
Especially stormy nights when the weather's foul,
They know that the wind sounds with a different howl.

The older children scare the younger ones
Sometimes—yet they too know the ancient fear.
They know sometimes that shrouded morning suns
Have shown grim proof the *Dyn Blaidd* has been near.
They've heard sometimes a gory river runs
Red in the dawn—and not from that black mere.

Especially when the moon shows his full face,
The local folk stay shuttered in their homes.
For legends tell of a cursed and evil race
That, when the moon is round, that valley roams.
Most days, most nights, they seem but normal souls,
But when *Dyn yn y Lleuad*** once more rolls
His wan face through the welkin's wide expanse,
Those out by lake or wood have little chance.

Of course the years have seen not one such beast—
Even those so accurst must one day die.
But those attacked would much prefer swift death,
Become the *Dyn Blaidd*'s bloody, grisly feast,
Than bitten—to live!—and thus be cursed for aye—
To dread each next full moon with every breath.

["Wolf Man" / **Man in the Moon"]

XXXIV
Pandemic

(a Bowlesian/Australian Sonnet)

They thought it could be easily contained—
That latest version of a "tool" for viral war.
But, after the breach, it was not long before
A tiny fraction of humanity remained.
Grim, vast, and loathsome herds of *The Undead*—
Yes, "dead" but reanimated, horrors—walk
And "turn" the living into *Them*. They stalk
Through urban streets and country roads. They spread
The awful blood contagion with their bite.
Infection means you have but a scant few days
Before you too will follow in the ways
Of plodding corpses—sleepless day and night.
   We living, here and there gathered, can but try
   To find some ways to stop them—*and not to die!*

XXXV
Weir Home
[after Poe]

(a Coffman Sonnet, Type 1* [Hybrid Sonnet] with irregular final couplet)

Nearby lies the small pond of Auber
  In a cirque the volcano has left.
  Midst trees withered, of leaves bereft,
We welcome this chill of October,
And we welcome the coming of night.
  For the night gives us freedom to roam
  From this region of mist and our home.
Dark of moon, stars obscured, bats in flight—
These are signs we are on the prowl.
  On such nights we come forth, sometimes near
  To your kind. Then you have more to fear
Than hoot of the owl or the wolves' howl.
  For we come for our feasting foul
  From the woodland *We* haunt—known as Weir.

XXXVI
The Witch House

(an English Sonnet)

Though it was called "The Witch House," we all knew
That Goody Hanks had died decades ago.
Still, there were strange tales of horror and grue
That had persisted. So, but few dared go
Near to the place—let alone to enter there!
But Seth and I knew of a cellar door
That was not latched. And so, on John Smith's dare,
We boys swore we'd go in—not just to explore,
But spend the night! How do I wish—my God!—
That we had not fulfilled that awful plan,
That we those halls bewitched had never trod—
Met her ghost there!—that Seth had lived to be a man!
  But I can't wipe that Face! from memory,
  Or horrors True—I'd thought could never be!

XXXVII
Preparations

(a Brisbane Sonnet)

I've come on ahead and made the voyage across,
Back home to London and secured the place
He'd paid much more for than I had advised.
Yet—as my client insists—it is "no loss
To have the perfect house secured apace,"
To quickly leave that realm he's long despised,
That region where his clan has been reviled.
He wishes, as he says, "A change of habitat.
"I have grown weary through these many years
Of these backward folk. And so I have exiled
Myself—chosen this 'Hub of Empire' that
O'erflows with Life—seek the company of my peers."

I've made all ready—preparatory toil.
Ah! here's my Master's coffin—lined with soil.

XXXVIII
Façade: Halloween Masked Ball—1925
(a Coffman Sonnet, Type 2V*; Coffman Sonnet, Type 1*; Coffman Sonnet, Type 6*; and Irregular Sonnet)

It was a full moon—indeed, a "blue moon" Halloween.
And, more than that, a huge moon at perigee.
I'm not sure how Charlie got me to agree
To attend the ball at the Biltmore in between
Our days at Brown's convention. I was tired.
And neither of us had costumes for the dance.

The "debate" was brief. As always, Charlie won.
But, at the bar, sat a woman who inspired
Friend "Chuck." Indeed, she was one to entrance!
Dressed all in black satin. Soon Charlie had begun
A conversation. He said, "I have to ask—
Did you devise that weird, wild costume that
You're wearing? And that most amazing mask!"
[A headdress all in black with the wings of a bat!]

I nursed my drink as Charlie worked his lines....
But it seemed more a question just who would seduce whom.
It wasn't long before they left for Charlie's room....
I'd seen this often enough, and I knew the signs.

I smiled and shook my head and finished my beer,
Then took the lift up to *the thirteenth floor.*
I fumbled with my keys when I found my door.
Though late at night, the dawn was nowhere near.

I was dog tired, but, once safely ensconced inside,
I donned my smoking jacket and, pipe alight,
Sat down to read a book. Then—tearing through the night,
From Charlie's adjoining rooms—his voice that cried:

"My God! Who...What are you?" Then—awful screams!
What happened next haunts almost all my dreams.

My side opened quickly, but his facing door was locked.
Not having the key, I had to force it wide.
No one could prepare for what I found inside!
I had thought myself a man not easily shocked.
    What had been Charlie lay there—a withered heap!
His body—*drained of blood they later found*!
    The woman wasn't there! But then—a sound!
I looked out the window….The sight still haunts my sleep.
There, clinging to the brickwork, but a few feet below—
 With long tongue licking off its bloody meal!—
A huge bat-thing! its fiery eyes aglow!
Then…off it flew! I swear the thing was real!
    Then voices: "What the Hell's going on in there?"
They barreled through the door. I could but stare.

    At first they thought I must have done the deed.
They had not seen those giant bat wings beating
'Gainst—fiend-eclipsed!—blood moon. It keeps repeating
In all my nightmares.
                        But the detectives had to heed
The testimony of several who had been
In rooms close by and one young man who'd seen
My friend and that weird woman dressed in black
Enter his room. Nor could they explain the lack
Of blood on my clothes, or the doctor's words who said,
    "Complete exsanguination! It's like he's been weeks dead!
That woman—somehow?—did this and then fled."
    It matters not if you believe my tale.
    But know, since then, when the deep Night is spread…
    I'm indoors, locked in and shuttered—without fail.

XXXIX
"Seek and Ye Might Find":
A Ghost Bloggers' Tale

(a Coffman Sonnet, Type 6*)

The old man had said, "Collecting data is one thing.
Observing strange phenomena should be your chore,
But be quite careful...for the very door
You might throw open—No telling what that might bring!
There is a difference between mortals who have passed
And other beings, far more dangerous than ghosts.
For, on that other side, are veritable hosts!
The powers of Evil are all there amassed."

They'd told him they would heed his sage advice.
But their viewers said they wanted "much more meat."
And that active place they'd dared to enter twice,
Had made their show go "virile." They would greet
A spirit there, named "Scratch," who claimed he knew
Dead ancestors. They reached out....He pulled them through!

XL
Out There

(a Coffman Sonnet, Type 1* [also called a Hybrid Sonnet])

The cosmic depths, though called so, are not "Void."
For that which we call "Space" is actually crammed
With Life in many forms: some blessed, some damned!
Beings near sentience, near thought, near extinct, destroyed!
Though "Time has ticked a Heaven round the stars."
Foul, Hellish Things are out there in *The Black*.
Our own world proves—of Evil there's no lack.
The pull of *It* is the horrid Truth that mars.

Ah, Yes! *They* are out there!—waiting in the dark—
Scanning near-infinite, open vasts of sky.
And we must hope they never will descry
Our small orb here. Hope they will never mark
This speck of dust. Hope they will never near
This world of ours—already fraught with Fear!

XLI
Loup-Garou
(an irregular sonnet in cross-rhymed duodecasyllabics)

The Beast is just a man most days, but then the moon
Will grow to full. And soon a grim change will unman
Whose path's by murder strewn—those curséd of that clan.
Since shapeshifting began and pentagramic rune
Appeared where his blood ran (for no one is immune,
None granted that sweet boon) red from that bite, nor can
He—doomed whene'er the moon is full, no longer wan—
Escape his plagued life's span, when round at midnight's noon
That orb hangs in the sky. 'Tis then the change begins,
And murders mount! His sins increase—and more shall die!

Thus does the *loup-garou*, the dreaded lycanthrope,
The cursed man-wolf sans hope, lose all that life he knew
When skies could still be blue. Ere this kaleidoscope
After each loathsome lope—gory ground and blood-red dew.

XLII
White Watkins

(English Sonnet, two Brisbane Sonnets, two English Sonnets, and a Brisbane Sonnet)

1.
"It was a weird, small, fanged, and furry creature,
But it wasn't any rat I can tell you!
It was dirty white in color, but the horrid feature
Was the weirdness of the face! I swear the view—
More than a fleeting glimpse—was of a small,
Yet *human* visage!—neither shrew nor rat.
And, just as terrible—more reason to appall!—
The thing, instead of paws had forelimbs that
Ended in *tiny hairless hands! Fingers and thumb!*
"What's that? No, Eliot, it's not 'bad dreams'—
Nor *Nightmares* rather! Two whiskeys can't benumb
My memory of the thing. Although it seems
Impossible, there's Something in that room
I rent—though Goody Watkins is long in tomb."

2.
"That ancient house up there on Henchman Street
Had rooms to let for, as they say, 'a song.'
And, on my student's budget, not much choice
Was open to me. And I chanced to meet
Fred Chapel up at school who tagged along.
We both took rooms—although an inner voice
Was whispering to me, 'No! Not this weird place!'
But I put by my apprehension. How
Could those old rumors possibly be true?
Though two-plus centuries did not erase
The legends of her hauntings there. And now
Perhaps it's her Familiar come in view!
I tell you, Eliot, I'm not insane
And Fred will tell you too. He's seen It plain!"

111

3.
  "Oh yes, I have had dreams—or hope they are!
There's Goody Watkins there and that cursed *Thing*.
In them that human-rat can even talk!
  Yes, Eliot, I know that most dreams are bizarre,
But the witch and that horrid *unfamiliar* bring
Me through deserted midnight lanes. We walk
Far out, far beyond any city street,
Beneath two moons! And very different skies!
We travel on through mist until we near
A tall figure in black—whom I *'must meet'*
They tell me—And then all Hope dies!
  And I am filled with abject, total fear.
Both witch and her white horror cower before
Dark Azathoth, who opens Chaos' door."

4.
  "I've read of him in that thrice damnéd book
That Miskatonic keeps—only God knows why!—
The Necronomicon. I dared to look
Into that tome that should be banned for aye!
  At first, it was to all my studies key,
But now my mind holds things I can't erase.
Those things I thought were simply myth—I see
Now *they were awful Truths of Cosmic Space!*
  "No, Eliot, I'm not mad; neither is Fred.
I tell you that white creature—from a hole
Chewed through my baseboard—poked its head
And spoke in tiny voice to chill my soul!
That foul, fanged, bearded face, with hideous sneer,
Intoned these words: 'Your very death is near!'"

5.

"'I am White Watkins and I bring my mistress' curse,'
That vile voice tittered. No! It was no dream!
I tell you, Eliot, it can get no worse.
Many horrors mount. *Things are not what they seem!*
   "Yes, what you suggest I have already begun—
Even though I know you think I'm not quite sane.
Both Fred and I, before tomorrow's sun
Will be moved out. We can no more remain
In that cursed place. My mind—my very soul!—
Depend on leaving that damned house, this town!
   "Believe me or not, that Witch House takes its toll
And will until they tear or burn it down.
   "At any rate, I'll keep in touch. I'll write.
I pray all will be well past this last night."

6. **Epilogue**

   The next day's paper held the grisly news
That two had died in a house on Henchman Street.
"Gruesome Murders": the large headline exclaimed.
Eliot read with horror, but the views
Of the police were sketchy, incomplete.
   So Eliot sought out three witnesses who were named.
The one who'd found Fred Chapel—or what remained—
Kept muttering, "The blood! God all the gore!"
The two who had gone up to his good friend's garret
Told him the floor, walls, ceiling—all were stained!
   "That poor lad's body! It's like something bore
Into his chest! And a blood-stained rat or ferret
Jumped out of him! and into a rat-hole in the wall!"
   But the other swore, "That waren't no rat at all!"

XLIII
Past Tense
(an irregular sonnet)

"The past never passes.
It simply amasses."
—Brad Leithauser

Though most may think the Present moment's all,
That our lives move through a flowing stream of Now,
We cannot hold tight any tock or tick,
Nor freeze one "frame" of Present. We don't know how.
The Future's seldom clear as moments crawl.
　　Though Near-"To-Come's" can often be previewed,
If we seek to peer much farther down that path,
The shapes are lost in haze first, then fog thick
Obscures, then solid wall blocks aftermath.
　　But, with the Past, there's little to occlude.

　　There we may travel; through Memory we may stay
And visit Places, Moments, Ghosts of those gone,
Reverse Time's cycle, trading dusk for dawn.
But—barriers down—may *They* also come *this way?*

XLIV
Joining the Club

(Coffman Sonnet, Type 2V, three Brisbane Sonnets)

1.

He was told the old wooden bridge across Long Creek
Was not a problem and would hold his truck.
He crossed it slowly. Every crack and squeak
Told him they lied—and it was only luck
That got him safely to the other side.
   But "The Club" was hidden down this old dirt road,
Narrow and winding, through that forest deep—
And they had told him that he must decide:
   "You want to be a member?" Ralph would goad.
"But, if you join, there are secrets you must keep."
   He rounded a bend, and the canopy overhead
Of crossing boughs of the winter-naked trees
Opened. And, just then, a sudden breeze
Shook limbs—but all else about seemed very dead.

2.

No lights were on within the log-built shack,
Two windows, one each side a central door,
Showed like black eyes, the door a rough-hewn maw.
At first, he thought of turning to go back,
But, just to learn directions there, he swore
He'd follow through.
                      "That's our first Law,"
Joe Quinn had said. "For you to even know
Just how to find us—there's no backing out.

115

Once you begin 'The Journey' (he'd made it sound
So mystical) you just plain gotta go
Through with 'The Test,' know what it's all about."
Well, he was here. There was no turning 'round.
　　Just then, the "eyes" lit up. He wasn't alone.
　　Then, from inside, he heard a muffled moan.

3.
　　He left his truck and walked up to the door,
Knocked three times quick, then a pause, then two more slow.
　　"Who knocks" (Ralph's voice).

　　　　　　　　　　　　　　　He replied, "A willing Brother"—
Just as he had been taught three days before.
The dark "mouth" opened. And, at first, a flashlight's glow
　Held right up to his face, and then—another.
　　"You tryin' to blind me! What the Holy Hell gives!"
　　"Be silent, Neophyte! Until one learns
Our ways one may not know the Dark,
The Laws that govern just who Dies or Lives,
Your eyes must know that Light is the Thing that Burns!
And Darkness is needed if you would embark
Upon The Journey you have sworn to tread.
Any Light upon that path's a thing to dread."
4.
　　Then Joe's voice, "Swear now you'll complete the task
Needed to join us as a Member here.
Swear that you'll keep our Secrets—on your Life!"
　　"I swear," he said. "I will do what you ask."
The lights cut out. In a corner, tied up in fear,
Was the reason they had told him, "Bring a knife."
Huddling there was some old, homeless bum.

He recognized him—from outside the liquor store—
Begging for coins for another pint of booze.
   Realizing what they expected made him numb
At first—But then he continued with the chore.
This sad life, after all, was nothing much to lose.

   The pleading, screams and bloody work all done,
He found he loved it! His new life had begun.

XLV
The Reaping

(an extended irregular sonnet)

He always took great pleasure in *the reaping*.
Each *harvest* proved that, through hard work,
Planning, and careful tending to the goal,
One could succeed—prove once again one's skill.
    For years he had devoted heart and soul
To nurturing his craft: just how to lurk,
How stalk, observe *them*—awake or sleeping.
    He gratified himself. Then smiled at the reverse
Of natural order that he brought about—
Gleaning before planting was the twist.
    This new one here was just another kill.
Another poor thing who would not be missed—
"Least not for a day or two. Them cops can't figure out
My methods. Hell! The papers say 'Perverse.'
That name-slinging won't get me to stop."
    Hole dug, *he added the new "seed" to his crop.*

XLVI
Captain Gruchy's Ghost:
A Tale of Old Boston's North End Tunnels

(an Irregular sonnet on slant rhymes, a "Kangaroo Pause" Sonnet, an English Sonnet)

1.

   Old Thomas Gruchy, famous "privateer"
(elsewise, less politely, known as "pirate"),
Picked one cold and gusty night to disappear,
But left—some say—vast treasures that he got
From raids upon French vessels in England's war.
   At any rate, there are very few who doubt
There's something beyond the eldritch, brick-sealed door
In the cellar of his queer old house on Salem Street.
   But why would Gruchy leave Boston town without
His smuggled loot?
               And some say you could meet—
Somewhere between that arch and Copp's Hill's tombs—
The Captain's ghost! For the tunnel wends that way.
And other darksome legends lower and loom
Above those carved-out depths that still hold sway.

2.

   Charles Pickman, for one, had a place on Commercial Street,
His cellar held a deep—some say "The Devil's"—well.
It too was covered, sealed so none might greet
Abominations from the depths of Hell.
   But Gruchy—so the fables all have told—
Amassed an amazing trove of curséd gold.
Now, unglittering in that gloom, are precious jewels.
But those who'd seek such mark themselves as fools.

There sits a small cenotaph atop Copp's Hill,
Marked with the initials *T.* and *G.*
Within, well-hidden, a marble trap door still
Awaits the searcher. *But best let it be!*
For far less would be found—and far more lost!—
In that corridor guarded by Old Tom's ghost.

3.
   For you see, the pirate Captain never left,
Nor did his stores of secret, stolen booty.
Oh yes, he'd planned to keep those fruits of theft,
All of his ill-got, *kill-got* wealth, the loot he
Had hoarded and stored below that old North street.
   But, as he was hefting chests onto a cart,
There were some *Things* in the gloom he chanced to meet—
Too horrid even for him! They stopped his heart!
   So, Thomas Gruchy's bones are still down there,
More rotten than that heart that could not take
The sight of Evils—more than mortal man can bear.
   Rats, corpse-worms, beetles, spiders make a grim wake,
Riding that bone-ribbed vessel—Old Tom their host!
But keeping Horror's hoard safe…is Gruchy's ghost.

XLVII
Words on Ghastly Vellum Writ

(two English Sonnets)

… Perturbe'd men that tremble at a sound,
And ponder words on ghastly vellum writ,
In vipers' blood, to whispers from the night—
Infernal rubrics, sung to Satan's might…
—George Sterling, from "A Wine of Wizardry"

Mostly unknown, there are some secret tomes
The words of which gloss totalities of Evil.
They hold forbidden chants and cryptic poems
Writ by the hands of those leagued with the Devil.
Some books, beyond the "Noonday Devil's" sway,
Contain such horrors from the Depths of Night,
From far beyond our tiny "Milky Way,"
From far beyond the Cosmos' farthest light.

Yet there are those among us who dare to ponder
Those ghastly words on human vellum writ,
Whose souls are doomed to some unholy yonder,
As they to Darkness and Chaos submit.
Beyond all Terrors of our mundane zone,
They beckon *Beings* who should ne'er be known.

With vile, infernal rubrics these grimoires
Contain foul conjurings and demonic spells
That call up Worldly Evils. But—beyond the stars—
 From a zone of Unimaginable Hells,
"*The Old Ones*" are summoned with their heinous spawn
To once again engulf our world in Dark
And Fears more fell than any cloudless dawn
Could hope to cleanse away.
                              Each loathsome mark
Set down in blood of vipers or—of men!—
Has power to motivate fey *Nameless Cults*
Who seek to summon *Them*, to call *Them* in,
Knowing full well the hideous results,
Seeking with black-hearted, blasphemous might
To bring the coming of that Endless Night.

XLVIII
Last Thoughts of the Amateur Medium

(an Rhymed Sestina Sonnet*)

"We cannot stay the coming of the night.
But now I know there are other kinds of Dark
More sinister by far and cause for dread!
Ah me! There is grim reason for my fright—
That *Thing* appeared and called out to me:

$$\text{'Hark!}$$

You have invoked a spell that wakes the Dead.
You sought to summon a loved one. But Instead
The Gate is open. I am Hell's Acolyte!
Not knowing the journey's end did you embark.
We, demons who bow to Evil's Patriarch,
May freely pass!'

$$\text{"And now I know my plight}$$

And know I'm cursed. Yes! I am doomed! I've led
The Demon here! I've fled, but just ahead O Horrid Sight!
My flight was all for naught! Mark *IT* there! Deathly stark!"

XLIX
Dawn of the Night
(a Korean Kasa Sonnet* [random head-rhymed rather than end-rhymed])

Far past the Void that we call "Space."
  There is a zone of Cosmic Dread.
    Chaos reigns there. But would rule here;
     They—Horrid thought!— seek to return
  Where once they dwelt—before expelled:
*Nyar*lathotep, Disorder's Lord,
    Spawn of Deep Dark, Dread Azathoth;
    Grim Yog-Sothoth who guards *The Gate*
  Who IS The Gate, from Nameless Mist
    Born long ago. And here on Earth,
    Lorn of all hope, we dwell for now,
  THEY strive to keep our threatened realm.
    Dim is that chance, for soon will come
    Dawn of that Night!—when Cthulhu wakes.

L
La Villa Infestada:
The Last Pages from The Journal
of Montague LeFanu Blackpool
(a sequence of Stornello Sonnets*)

1.

"Looking back, I still ask, 'How was I to know?'
That villa on the hill had a wondrous view
Of that valley where stretched out the River Po.

It had seemed the perfect place for my retreat—
From This World, yes—but also *Another* that
I'd sought to enter, not knowing what I'd meet!

But I had entered. My God! the horrors met
If one crosses that threshold! And I cannot
Drive them from my mind—though I yearn to forget.

Foolishly, I thought, 'Here…here I will be free
From fell fiends that from *that Nether Zone* did fly.'
I should have known They'd have ways to follow me!

Oh yes, there was brief span—a few bright weeks….
But a Demon, soon or late, finds what it seeks.

2.

"The days were warm, but shade and evenings cool.
September was crawling onward toward the fall.
It seemed my plan had worked. But I was a fool!

On the equinox—a wild and stormy night—
It became clear that the cursed *Forbidden Gate*
I had sought to close again had not shut tight.

The spells I had found in that accursed grimoire
Had worked too well! They had opened wide *The Door*,
And *Beings* emerged! Some banished long of yore.

I had succeeded by other chants and spells
To send most back to the deepest, blackest Hells.
But soon I learned it matters not where one dwells.

My meddling magic could not be taken back;
My mere living on had left a trail to track!

3.
"So I've fled my hoped for refuge on the hill
From my villa to the village church. But still
I know *my Nemesis* follows—always will!

I seek unlikely hope of sanctuary
Here in this holy place, yet I am wary.
I know no balm can heal *This Sin* I carry.

Father Medici, man of wisdom and grace,
Went up to the villa to exorcise the place.
I cannot forget the look upon his face….

When he returned it was well into the night.
He told me his ministrations had been for naught.
'The Evil in that place is more than cause for fright!

My Son, I fear I know not what to do;
I've never met such *Powers* that now plague you.

4.
" 'I will send word to a friend I have in Rome,
The most successful exorcist of our time.
Perhaps he can undo spells from that cursed tome.'

. . .

Today we spent in silence and in prayer
In hopes that the Demon could not enter here.
Thus, we've done all we can think of to prepare.

. . .

But now the black night has come. All light has sped.
Looking out, there are no bright stars overhead....
In the chapel...Oh, Dear God! The priest lays dead!

. . .

Now I've locked myself into this cellar room,
This dark, dank place befitting the name of 'tomb.'
So ends my tale it seems—a much deserved doom....

It comes!
        Dear Soul, If you read this, understand
Why I chose, at last, a death by my own hand."

LI
El Coco

(a Septilla Sonnet [Spanish Septets]*)

Most think it's just a legend meant to scare
The young into behaving. A Nightmare
Folktale that parents very long ago
Made up to frighten children to obey,
Lest they be eaten!—or spirited away
To someplace that the living do not know.
Yet cannibal *El Coco IS* out there!

From the high rooftops It can scan and peer
Through doors and windows, searching all the town,
Shapeshifting Shadow, but—when it slinks down—
The Chosen has no chance as It draws near!
Most doubt this tale, Yet *El Coco is real!*
Unruly children make a grisly meal.
This fiend is ample reason for stark Fear.

LII
Santa Compaña

(an Espinela Sonnet sequence*)

1.
Now come again the Ancient Host,
Estantigua. "Tormented Dead,"
In grim procession, are now led
Down village paths. *They are The Lost!*

Now at midnight each harried Ghost
Follows behind a living man.
White-hooded all—although few can
See the candle-bearing spirits.
But living souls who come near its
Passing close by must have a plan:

Solomon's Seal! They quick must trace
The Hexagram into the dust
Within a Circle, and they must
Lay down in it and hide the face.

2.
He who leads them carries a curse:
A trance takes him at each midnight
To lead this weird *Parade of Fright*
Through towns and forests, but there's worse....

He must each night this plague rehearse
With no memory in the morn
That he has led across the *Bourn*
Of Death that sad, lost multitude.
Holy Water or Holy Rood
He carries to guide these Hope Forlorn.

But neither Cross nor Water Pure
Can serve to take away Their sins.
Each midnight it again begins.
For Leader's Curse there's but one cure:

3.
The Living Man will not live long
Unless he find one unwary
Other who'll take up and carry
Water or Cross and join the throng.

To any who might come along
The Curse, the Trance will transferred be,
But most folk, though they cannot see
The white-clad, hooded Dead can tell—
As warm wind wafts and candle's smell
Come to them—they in danger be.

And so, face down, *they prostrate lie*
In Starred Circle, or they can make
The Horn Sign—and two fingers take:
First and little finger defy.

4.
When this sad procession goes by,
All shiver, shudder—sudden chill
Comes o'er them. But a rare few will
See the *Compaña* and descry

The dim, pale Shades of those who die
Unshriven or in Darkest Sin.
Some others see faint glimmers when
They pass; their Ghost Lights skim along
The night's long shadows. *That Lost Throng*
Comes through each night that *Veil* too thin.

This grim passing will oft portend
That Death for someone soon is near.
All the more reason for stark Fear!
For these processions have no end.

LIII
As Summer Turns to Autumn

(a Latvian Daina Sonnet*)

Now as Summer turns to Autumn,
On this eve of ancient Samhain,
We are those, the ones who gather,
Practicing the ancient rituals.

See the towering bale-fire blazing;
See the embers flying skyward;
See the Sacrifice we offer;
See the Priest with golden dagger.

Blood we offer up at Midnight.
Drugged and bound upon the altar
Lies the Gift that must be given,
So the land give forth its bounty.

Thus it has been through the ages,
Mother and Green Man, claim these wages.

LIV
Baleful Bond
(a sonnet using the Welsh meter of Byr A Thoddaid*
and the harmony of Cynghanedd Sain*)

Tales told it was demon-haunted,
But we two remained undaunted.
And the oath that we both swore was our bond,
Beyond any Power—
Spectral or Earthly—we would stay
In that house 'til dawn the next day.
Fear grew as we drew near. The moon was new.
Nether Dark gave us pause…
But within minutes we were in.
It did not take long to begin!
A brief lull. Then a dull sound we heard. Dread
Deepened. And then—one word:
                                        "Die!"
I screamed and into the night I flew!
I knew—with my friend's death!—those Tales are true!

Frank Coffman

LV
Grammy Hawkins' Book
(Coffman Sonnet, Type 2V*)

He was the last survivor of this line,
So "Great Grammy Hawkins" house came down to him.
He thought, "At last! This place is finally mine!"
He'd fallen on hard times, his prospects dim.
"But now, I'll sell it for a goodly sum!"
His fortunes had finally turned. He began to explore
The huge, old mansion high atop Proctor's Hill.
He had no notion of the Fate to come
When he finally forced his way through that locked door
And found the odd, ancient tome that Grammy's will
Had promised 'could fulfill one's every desire.'
He began to read by the lantern's leaping light—
Then he knocked it over! Fleet flames cut off his flight!

None could explain how a book survived that fire.

LVI
Poenari

(A Canopus Sonnet in Alexandrines, with variant second septet*)

Above the valley where the River Argeș cuts
Through the Southern Carpathians a fearsome fortress stands.
High on a craggy point that curséd castle juts
Its fanglike towers skyward. It is known in many lands
As "Castle Dracula," that citadel inspires
Legends most vile and foul. That heinous height commands
Dark, deep-wood vistas. Tales of Impalings and Vampires.

Count Vlad Dracul, "The Dragon's Son," ruled from those heights.
Though many of his Romanian countrymen revere
His memory as Defender of the West, pure Fear
Is palpable at that place. And some folk say at nights
His *Strigoi* brood—and Yes! even Vlad himself! roam round
That Transylvanian stronghold and all grim lands near.
What's certain is some who dare that zone...are never found.

Frank Coffman

LVII
The Unlikeness

(a Webb Sonnet, form proposed by poet Don Webb*)

The old house had been vacant thirty years.
 She wondered at that…and the price—so very low?
But the place was roomy, kept up. Any fears
Were allayed. She loved "the feel" of long ago.

The first week: dusting, painting, mopping floors.
Then, curious, she went down the basement stairs.
Old bed frames, piles of books, but Oh! That mirror!
A full-length fine antique with oaken frame.
With care, she took it upstairs to her room.
At first, a reflection of her youth abloom
Showed back. But then—*uncanny changes came!*
The image was an old crone! And…coming nearer…
Another! A *Thing* more ghastly than her worst nightmares!
Her last screams echoed through that House of Horrors!

LVIII
Breed Accursed
(a Tercetina Sonnet*)

Around these somber rows of incised stones
In this old graveyard, as harsh autumn cools
The land, there lurks a horrid, hell-born breed.

Foulest of all foul fiends, their gruesome need
Is violation of the dead, eat flesh, gnaw bones!
Abhorent harvest, breaking all of Nature's rules.

Ass-hooved, wolf-jawed, they are the Ghouls!
Loathsome they live and blasphemously feed,
Coming forth nightly from their nether zones.

Wind moans o'er chill pools. Take thee heed!

They breathe from foul maws their pestilential breath,
After feasting on the cursed food that they crave—
Despoilers of the hoped-for quiet grave.
Yes, there are horrors worse, by far, than Death!

Frank Coffman

LIX
Chaos from the Cosmos

(a Curtal Sonnet using G.M. Hopkins' "Sprung Rhythm")

Chaos! Coming from the Depths of a Cosmos Vast-
er than even the broadest Imagination can conceive,
The Old Ones design to once again hold us under their sway—
As *They* had done, eons long gone in the dim, dark past,
Remembered by none, but in which many believe.
And some among us—deranged!—*who long for such a day!*

Names of that host, names that should never be spoken
Though known: Cthulhu, Azathoth, Nyarlathotep…would cleave
Our sane world asunder, wring horrors upon us so vast none can say
How deep the terrors that might be wrought. Our World broken!
Fear Them!

LX
Curse of the Undead
(a Miltonian Caudate Sonnet)

The time rolls on. Fully six hundred years
That he has roamed as one of *The Undead!*
How many thousands he has slain or bled
To turn them too?…His memory slowly blears.
Among the vile *stregoi* he has no peers;
His vampire spawn have thus heinously spread
Unholy contagion. Their pestilence has led
To tales that invoke the greatest of our fears:

To lose one's very soul! The price they've paid
For that false immortality. Grim death
Dispensed to those…lucky to simply die
And not be changed—into a vampire made!
Foul *nosferati!* Innocents lose the Breath
Of Life! On vital blood these fiends rely.

A bat in the darkling sky,
A thing that prowls, seeming part wolf, part man,
A human in form, but fanged!—these things can
Reveal this horrid clan!
Beware! Never skoff at this worldwide belief!
To meet *The Undead* means death or eternal grief!

Frank Coffman

LXI
Beyond the Bourn
(an experimental sonnet—
an English Sonnet using 5342 accent lines in the quatrains
with a regular pentameter couplet*)

When one, sans breath, is borne beyond that bourn
The Mystery is solved.
That one, twixt Earthly morn to morn,
Is not involved—
At least no more in this zone to sojourn
(So goes the common thought)
But we, the living, sometimes learn
That such is not
The case for all who go *Beyond The Veil!*
Yes! Some of those souls return:
Murdered, possessed, vengeful may not fail
That change to spurn.
And so full many phantom entities
Come back to plague us here—or seek for peace.

Frank Coffman

LXI
Beyond the Bourn
(an experimental sonnet—
an English Sonnet using 5342 accent lines in the quatrains
with a regular pentameter couplet*)

When one, sans breath, is borne beyond that bourn
The Mystery is solved.
That one, twixt Earthly morn to morn,
Is not involved—
At least no more in this zone to sojourn
(So goes the common thought)
But we, the living, sometimes learn
That such is not
The case for all who go *Beyond The Veil!*
Yes! Some of those souls return:
Murdered, possessed, vengeful may not fail
That change to spurn.
And so full many phantom entities
Come back to plague us here—or seek for peace.

141

LXII
The Woman of the Mound
(A sonnet in an approximation of Irish *Snam Suad* meter*)

"More than wail of the gale"—is the tale's history.
There is more at the core of the lore's mystery.
At that sound, all around understand, fearfully:
From the mound She is bound thus to keen mournfully.
It means Death! And the breath will soon leave a mortal,
Flesh and bone, someone known in the zone, through a portal
Will soon leave. Others grieve, but cannot do a thing
And the cost—the one lost will be ghost on the wing.
If one sees 'neath the trees an old crone in the night
Crouching there, long grey hair, red eyes glare—gives a fright!
But her voice! There's no choice but to be terrified!
For you see—it is She, the Banshee—verified.
Deathly pale, at her wail, without fail, one is doomed.
Horrid cry! One will die! One nearby soon entombed.

LXIII
Perspective
(An English Sonnet)

"Ah! more *Warm Ones* have arrived today!
More precious energy to shock and drain!
We must be careful to prolong their stay—
To feed our need as long as they remain.
It has been too long since *The Living* occupied
Our darkened house. So many long, cold years
Our cravings—our lust for the essence—been denied.
Now, once again, *we may feed upon Their fears!*

"Look! How *The Young One* senses us gathered here!
She tells *The Woman* she doesn't 'like this place.'
It has already begun. *Smell the delicious Fear!*
It shows in The Child's—and now...The Woman's face!
Let us begin to plan for this first night...
Just how to begin, to prolong this *Feast of Fright!*"

LXIV
The Fiend of The Fens
(A sonnet in the Welsh Meter of Cywydd Deuair Hirion*)

A dire span—water and sand—
Marks a zone in East England.
At night, in fog, that baleful bog
Writes many a sad epilogue.
Foul and fell that curséd Fen.

A weird wight has awoken—
A *Thing* that moves…although dead!—
And that dread marsh infested.
Those who come too close are caught
By that phantom's fierce onslaught!
Tales are told by some who've come
Upon gory sights most gruesome!
There have been many who went
Too near and now are silent.

LXV
Cornish Creatures
(a sonnet based upon Cornish 14th c. hexains*)

There are three fabled wights of Cornwall:
Bucca, Knockers, and the *Spriggans* small.
Bucca Dhu, black sea sprite, stirs the storm.
Fishermen leave shoreline offerings.
   Spriggans, wizened dwarfs, once giant kings,
Blight crops, leave changlings in horrid form
To plague our ilk, raise the whirlwind,
Harry travellers.
            Where tin is mined
   The *Tommyknockers,* grim fiends to dread,
Signal dire cave-ins with knocks and creaks,
So miners leave food for these small freaks
At mine mouths.
           Better these three are fed
Than their mischief grows the number dead—
These creatures who plague our humankind.

LXVI
Citadel Accursed
**(from *The Expedition Journal of
Ambrose Algernon Drummond*,
Posthumously Published
London: Polidori & Lee, 1893.
[detailing events of 19-22 September 1888])**
(a sequence of Welsh Gwawdodyn Sonnets
using the cynghanedd "harmonies" of draws, sain, and lusg*)

1.

"That castle infamous was our quest.
To assail that rough trail was a test.
The way before us ran through vast forests,
One hundred miles north of Bucharest.
  "That Citadel was deemed a Hell-gate.
Local folk signed the Cross and our fate
They forewarned: 'Oh, Good Sirs, you must not go!
You do not know what horrors await!'
  From the outset, our plan was to find
All weird truths of that place so maligned,
The ruins of Dracul's Poenari,
And if he was the *Scourge of Mankind*—
An undead monster as the tales told,
Or but the 'Impaler' of legends old.

2.
    "We were determined, yet we had doubt:
'What are all these wild stories about?'
We'd explore. What was more, we swore we'd stay
As long as needed in that redoubt.
    Smith, Ervin, Pierce, Van Helsing and I
Approached those ruins hung in the sky.
Steep, cruel, and grueling the path to our goal,
That dour, gray, grim fortress perched on high.
    Far below the Argeş River flowed,
A thin ribbon as the sunset glowed,
Like a flood of blood in the vale below.
    As night fell, we reached the Count's abode.
Six centuries since those stones had been laid;
Nearly five since Vlad's legend had been made.

3.
    "We reached the ruins as the last ray
Shone on the stone walls and steep stairway,
Knifing through one gap in gathering clouds.
Night's shroud and fierce storm cloaked that decay.
Pierce led our way to a sheltered room.
    As lightnings forked through deepening gloom,
One could catch a glimpse of crumbling spires—
Between bolts, the dark of the tomb was ours.
    The tallest tower of that lofty keep
Loomed o'er the river. Vertical steep
Was the huge drop down to the Argeş' stream.
The tower from which Vlad's wife would leap
When the Ottoman horde arrived that day
As Count Vlad Tepes battled far away.

4.
   " 'Better to be crushed and food for fish
Than taken by Turks!' was her last wish.
So went the tale. Then she leapt to her death.
   But the bards all say—'Twas not her finish.
Her ghost still haunts the valley below.
And local peasants attest it is so:
   'She moves through the forest or near the shore
In torn gown. her spirit, wraithlike, aglow.'
   'Yes! A weird green light glints all around
Her cursed ghost. She floats, not touching ground!'
   'A lucky few have seen her and lived;
Unlucky many found dead or not found.'
   'She is but one of the fell phantom hosts:
Impaled men, lost soldiers, Vlad's slaves—all ghosts!'

5.
   "That stormy night we sat round the fire
Smith had made with the wood from a spire
That had collapsed clearly long years before.
We retold the wife's tale. And of Vlad's ire.
   Defending the Faith, Dracul had won.
But, with his wife's death, that Faith was undone.
'Is this my reward?!' He turned from his God.
He gave up his soul. Stark Evil had won!
   The legend told that he made a pact
Then with the Devil—an awful act.
Though dead he'd be *Undead* eternally.
That was the tale. But what was the fact?
That was the question we'd sworn to pursue.
Was Vlad a vampire? The stories true?

6.
  "On the morn, we began inspections.
One could see leagues in all directions:
A great sylvan wilderness sprawled below;
Argeş' crawled through in serpentine flow.
  That first day we all worked to insure
Our 'room' less a tomb, more intact.
We worked to make sure that we were secure
So we might endure whatever attacked:
Whether it be what foul weather wrought,
 Or some actual *strigoi's* onslaught
(Though the latter we doubted. At that stage
'Twas a likelihood none of us thought.)
  By that second night we were well prepared
Long before a blood-red sunset flared.

7.
  "While Van Helsing had researched Vlad's tale,
Smith and Erwin brought tools to assail—
If weird lore was true, they felt sure they knew
What arcane methods might best prevail:
If legends proved to be factual,
If Vlad—or his monstrous ilk—actual;
Holy water, crosses, stakes of wood,
Could, as would Bibles, prove tactical.
Each wore a chain with a crucifix
About his neck—'twas thought to transfix
All vampiric creatures, those damned by God,
Denied any chance to "Cross the Styx"—
(To phrase it in an ancient metaphor);
Never could that foul brood gain *The Far Shore*.

8.
"Our wait was not long. Just at midnight
We beheld a form, a spectral wight,
A woman gowned, with a ghostly green glow
Surrounding her shape, an eerie sight.
   Then she spoke. Her first word drawn out: 'Who-o-o-o
Are ye who would dare enter here? You
Dare to enter my Master's citadel!
What you have done you cannot undo.'
   Then her form faded into the mist
Of midnight, but her voice did persist:
   'Hark! My Master now comes! None shall be spared!'
My God! She foretold an unholy tryst.
For out of the high tower's door there came
The Thing! He spoke: *'Dracul is my name.'*

9.
"Corpse-pale his face; his arms spread his cape
Like huge bat wings. His fanged mouth agape,
He floated toward us! I swear it is true.
And for poor Ervin there was no escape!
Bravely, he held a crucifix high
But he stood transfixed as *It* came nigh.
As if mesmerized, Ervin dropped the cross
And silently offered his neck—to die!
   Then the vampire raised both arms. And lo!
Our room's wall collapsed! The valley below
Would now be the tomb of friends Smith and Pierce,
So fierce was the onslaught of that *Prince of Woe.*
Van Helsing and I, down the central path
Ran to escape that foul *strigoi*'s wrath.

150

10.
 "Our descent from that height remains unclear
In my mind. But the sense of abject Fear
Will remain with me always, I've no doubt.
But one more Horror would then appear!
    When we reached the wild-wood land below.
We saw, through the trees, an eerie glow!
In gossamer gown, bloody with gore,
Tattered and torn, forlorn did *She* flow
Through that forest of dread, *Vlad's spectral wife!*
She who, in despair, had given up life
And flung herself to the valley below—
Now to roam a ghost in grim afterlife.
    She beckoned to us, Van Helsing and I,
But we to the village hastened to fly.

11.
 "I swear to God that this tale is true—
Weird as it is for one to construe!
Five went to research a tale. Only two
Came back from that journey I shall rue
To my dying day—which is likely near,
For, since my flight from that Castle of Fear,
Hounded by a keen sense of foreboding,
My strength has waned with each passing year.
    Van Helsing still lives, sworn to strive on
To end that *Fiend* and his *Strigoi Spawn.*
I pray that friend Abraham will not fail
In that quest—usher in a New Dawn,
Hold Count Dracula and his ilk at bay,
That living Mankind know a brighter day."

LXVII
Problem Dis-Solved
(A Rimas Dissolutas Sonnet*)

"Of proving possible invisibility
Of biologic matter, the early tests
Upon my formula are encouraging…"
His journal notes: *"I'm quite sure I'm now capable!"*
It is now clear he used himself as subject.
The journal: *"The experiment is going well…"*
But later entries show a sickened brain.

"Both soft tissues and bone show sensitivity
But all my work upon this last dose rests!…"
Then: *"Dear God! The virus uses blood for nourishing!"*
The horrid truth was now quite inescapable:
What he'd unleashed left him a shriveled object!

They could not see the gore, but Oh! The smell!
To find it on the floor they used red stain.

LXVIII
A Place Possessed
(An Englyn Cyrch-Terza Rima Sonnet,
Blending Welsh and Italian Forms*)

The rumors about that place
Have spread wide over the years.
There are fears none can erase.
It is said a *Death's Head* peers
Out from a window upstairs,
And bares sharp fangs as it leers
At any who dares, who fares
Near to that house of Horror—
Let alone explore! For there's
Lore—one bold soul swore that gore,
Gruesome gouts covered the walls
And floors! Halls dreaded from yore
All should shun. All should beware!
Scant hope for any who enter there.

LXIX
Beyond All Hallows'
(a Clogyrnach Sonnet using some
of the Welsh Harmonies—Cynghanedd:
Sain, Lusg, and Draws)

The Eve of All Hallows' has passed:
That long night of horrors amassed.
But the atmosphere
Of that time of year—
Evil's Sphere...
     is still vast.

Know there linger long past that night
Full many fell reasons for fright.
You should have no doubt
Such Things are about
That drown out
     Reason's might.

Such grim Truths can drive one insane!
In tatters leave matters mundane.

LXX
Laplace's Demon

*"We may regard the present state of the universe
as the effect of its past and the cause of its future."*
— Pierre-Simon Laplace, *A Philosophical Essay on Probabilities*

(a Coffman *Italian Megasonnet**—in long syllabic lines)

One could predict the fall of scoundrel Michael Laplace.
From his youth, he was every debauch's very epitome.
So much unlike his great uncle, the scholar Pierre-Simon,
Michael Laplace was far, far removed from Intellect's throne.
No one objectively observing his acts could fail to see
That his deeds were so heinous that he had no hope of Grace.

He persisted in grievous Sins on a predetermined line.
When he embraced the Occult, turned in the Devil's direction,
The projection of all: "He is damned! There is no hope for his soul!"
When he found a fell grimoire, and conjuring became his goal,
All knew that his path was clear!—he would suffer Demonic Infection!
Yet there are still some who doubt the Cosmos' Great Design.

The course of his life was determined; his ending had been predictable.
Indeed, when they found him dead, saw that countenance of Horror,
All were sure they had judged it right; to think not would be a delusion.

The Ways of the Cosmos were clear; all outcomes were ineluctable.
The Future would follow from Now; all Now had sprung from Before—
Just as Michael's great uncle observed: Every Past had a foregone conclusion.

True. No Accident or Chance had made Michael's soul inflictable.
Yet many will say: "'Twas Free Will led him to the Devil's Door";
Or that: "Chaos is still the King." Over Fate—there is still confusion.

LXXI
The Devil's Dell
(an Awdyl Gywydd Sonnet*)

In a hidden upland dell
beings from Hell are invoked;
Weird, sub-human folk are led
in chants by priests in red cloaked.
Words framed in no earthly tongue
echo among the dark trees
that line the steep mountain slopes
that envelop that place. Breeze
cold and foetid fouls that zone,
to chill the bone, the throat choke.
Then, into their midst, a lone
sacrifice is shown. The smoke
from the summoned demon's rising is thick.
The victim's death is anything but quick.

LXXII
Eclipse of the Moon
(an Irregular Sonnet—in Hexameters*)

On those rare weirding nights with our moon in full eclipse,
When the "Old Man's Face" is stained and frowns down—red as blood!—
And shadows lengthen in the ruddy glow that's cast
Over our world, we gaze up. But without the dread that past
People—in heights of Terror through Time's long ebb and flood—
Looked at that Eaten Moon.
                                        Unknown the roughly circular ellipse
That Kepler and later Newton with Science—seeming certainty—
Made "clear": the mystic movements of the Deepest Skies.

But untold generations of the "We" down here,
Explained through myth and magic these wonders that we see.
We dare to think those Old Truths are just primitive lies,
And we dismiss them utterly—their Awe, their Fear.

Late or soon—like the moon—Our Eclipse! Whence we come; whither go?
And We will learn—at the last—what the past trillion souls all know.

OTHER GENRES, *HOMMAGES,* METAPOETICAL, & TRADITIONAL POEMS (AND A FEW MORE WEIRD ONES)

Micro-Organisms

(a Folk Ballad Sonnet*)

Would we be hideous to them—
Horror show monstrosities—
If they had minds that could hold Terror
Or that brave sense that sees?

Some even serve us in strange ways;
Some kill us with dread disease.
But there's no idea of Right or Wrong
In their DNA's strange keys.

They've no Mind to hold an Evil thought
Or plan a heinous deed;
Of course, no Soul to save or loose,
No Consciousness, Pride, or Greed;
No plan to deceive, nor a heart to break—
Unlike our Macro seed.

Little Armored One
With a nod toward Ogden Nash

There is a funny looking fellow;
His name is Spanish: *"Armadillo."*
The name means "little armored one."
One wonders how they have their fun?
They certainly aren't beauteous creatures—
Only mother armadillos could love their features.

A Ditty on One Rhyme

I'm Not Alone as One Prone
to Roam within the Echo Zone.
While some *vers librists* won't condone
my rhyming, I am not alone.
The free verse ilk have gen'rally eschown
these *sound* effects I seek to hone
[they're not for every Jack and Joan].
Their tone suggests that I postpone
true inspiration—that I clone
the chimes of elders and dethrone
organic form!
                          Such pure cornpone!
For—seeking rhymes—mickle thoughts are sewn.
that fill forms serendipitously shone.
As a *verser,* I strive for echoes of my own.

In Rome, they marked each calend, ide, and none.
We ride a roan pony that we have on loan.

Margin-Ail-ia

One should only pages "bleed"
In the case of direst need.
When some fine art must fill the page,
Margins and Headers might enrage.
So if one has nice art to show,
Then, by all means, let margins go.
But when the page the text must utter,
Be sure to give an ample gutter.
Margins and "ledding" meet the needs
Of readers. Care for one who reads.
Be kind! Don't let the crease devour
The artful words of writer's power.
And outside margins--also ample—
Will allow a joyful sample.
The reader will be thankful for it.
And woe to those who will ignore it.

Frank Coffman

Ousting Articles

(an Illini Sonnet*)
"If you can catch an adjective—kill it!"
—Mark Twain

   The articles are overused
By poets both of verse and those averse
To formal rhyme and measures—(strict or loose).
Though readers will rarely be confused
When "a(n)" or "the" they must traverse.
   Far better words will able poets use
In their sad, plodding stead *to vivify*
Their lines.
           One should avoid their curse.
If caught, "kill adjectives" said Twain—
But their potentials he would not deny.
While many should be by righteous edit slain,
An inspired spark might well educe
Apt word to well reward the poet's pain,
"Live" word for dull will be the line's great gain.

Poeti in grado di catturare gli strani
[Poets capable of capturing the strange]

(a Dantean Canzone Sonnet*
patterned after Dante's Canzone 1 in *La Vita Nuova*)

"…though I sang in my chains like the sea."
—Dylan Thomas

You poets who can catch the weird and strange,
Of my own craft I modestly would write.
Not to show all the many shades of Night,
But to explain two weirding ways of mine.
    Thus, I maintain it's no fault to arrange
One's length of verse or use full final rhymes.
    Nay! cadence regular and echoing chimes,
If sought and labored for, can well refine.
Not only writ—but finely wrought—each line,
Through stark surprise or serendipity,
Framed well by form, sets versifiers free.
    Like music's bars, strict lines do not confine.
If worked with heart and wit, a poem remains—
Though the wild wright who worked it sang in chains.

Frank Coffman

On Getting Older
(with a nod to A. E. Housman)

My birth month comes again. It's June.
Each year it seems it comes too soon!
Again the fields and woods are green,
And Life springs where the frost had been.

Now of my years—ten and threescore—
I've already made it through two more!
With how many more will I be blessed?
God only knows. But I shan't rest.

And summer suns and summer moons
Make me look forward to more Junes.
Fall's hues, springs sprung, even winter's blast
I'll cherish too—as in years past.

Long Lines of Gray
Heroic Futility at Gettysburg

(a Couplet Sonnet in Alexandrines)

"They've reinforced both flanks, so the center must be thin.
And though they hold the high ground, I have faith in our men."
"But, Sir, remember Fredericksburg. Now the enemy has the wall!
And wave on wave attacked and died. General Lee, you must recall.
There's near a mile of open ground and a long fence row to cross.
I greatly fear a massive charge will lead to massive loss!"
"I hear your cautions clearly, my good 'Old Warhorse,' Pete,
But we've come North to battle them and, ultimately, defeat
These foes who've plagued our Southern soil for more than two long years.
No. *You* remember Chancellorsville. Old friend, allay your fears."

And so near thirteen thousand men, formed in long lines of gray,
Charged up that deadly stretch of ground, but could not win the day.
And more than half of those who dared that gory stretch of ground
Beneath long lines of grey, grim stones those brave men can be found.

A Short Note to My Son:
—for Dean
(an irregular sonnet)

As in many "talks" fathers have with sons,
Likely what I'll say you've learned before.

"Learn what you seek. Then stay on track."

"The winning's not in how fast one runs,
But knowing just *Why* you're running is more."

"To persevere is all—succeed or fail—
With every bend in your own journey's trail,
Though troubles may arise 'round any turn."

"Though there'll be times the Wind is at your back,
There'll be many a time you'll face the gale."

"The task is to push on with a will to prevail,
For each of Life's wounds, to earn or to learn—
Through every bruise, cut, or knick—a knack."

"To sail Into the Wind…know how to tack."

Longmire
[An Hommage to a Newborn Legend]
(an irregular sonnet)

In Absaroka County, Walt Longmire
Walks tall across Wyoming's rugged land.
A man with nerves of ice and soul of fire,
Who sheriffs with a firm, yet gentle hand.
A man who understands the Cheyenne's plight,
Who understands the Goodness of plain folk,
Who knows just how to judge the Wrong, the Right,
And stands firm, tall and sturdy—like an oak.

We need to see more men of Longmire's like,
Strong guardians of the Just, defenders true,
Who are the Watchers, letting me and you
Live free, at peace when Evils seek to strike.
Yes, there are some who are quite big on talk—
But strong Walt Longmire always walks the walk.

Frank Coffman

The Nachtkrapp
["Night Raven"]
(a Balassi Sonnet* inspired by the poetic form, the Balassi Stanza**)

This horror tale is told in far-flung regions old
Of the *Nachtkrapp*—thing to dread!
List! Of this bugbear hear. Don't, when this fiend comes near,
Dare look at its wings or head!
One glance at absent eyes, holes in wings when it flies,
And you'll soon fall ill or dead!
After the twilight hour, it will catch and devour
Any children who are not abed,
Those who have strayed outside—those, as it may betide—
Whose path into bleak night led.

 Huge bird-thing, nature's laws defiled in beak and claws,
Rips off young limbs—then the heart
Is plucked in savage, horrid haste, and only gore
Is left in the nest. Each part
That once was human child—so late pure, meek, and mild—
GONE! *This caution I impart.*

Laika
(Лайка)

(an irregular sonnet)

Ten myriad generations from the wolf,
Ages of faithfulness to our imperfect race,
One dog was chosen to test out that gulf,
The true "first step" into the near void of space.
True, a veritable kennel had gone before,
An experimental, but sub-orbital "pack."
Most were brought "home" alive, but she would soar
Out into orbit—no plan to bring her back.
Once more to "serve" Mankind, we would depend
Upon a dog, sailing—before her journey's end—
Beyond where no living thing on Earth could climb.
Free from the capsule, no more cage, no bars:
One pebble tossed into the Sea of Time;
One tiny spirit rippling through the stars.

Frank Coffman

This Side

(a Ballade Supreme, a Refrain Double)

The *Unknown* is dubbed the strongest form of Fear,
Attested by many souls accounted wise.
But when into the *abnatural* we peer,
When this world's laws are broken, we surmise
That when the thought-impossible near us nighs—
Shaking all Reason—when something "bumps" the night,
When things that can't be seen come into sight,
When all our notions of Reality fail
And *something dreadful* obscures Logic's light,
We're left to ponder what's *Beyond the Veil.*

The old tales tell that some are with us here—
Beings of legend. And our Reason vies
Against the notion such wights might be near,
Let alone extant, so our mind denies
The possibility. But our surety dies
When we encounter *what just can't be Right!*
And fully "Known" the reasons for our flight,
Before which things we cannot help but quail.
Those *present* Fears are stronger far, despite
Our need to ponder what's *Beyond the Veil.*

And, though most cherish Life as that most dear,
We all have wondered just what it is that lies
Beyond that *Curtain* that even the sagest seer
Cannot foretell—*that last supreme surprise.*
Though there be creeds that claim we shall arise
From this, our universal earthly plight,
We, generally, have no wish to expedite
Such transformation—head into that gale
That blows from that dim region or invite
The proof of that which lies *Beyond the Veil.*

Know there are things that reach Fear's greatest height!
The *Summum Terrorum* that stark horrors excite,
Things against which Reason cannot prevail,
That blight us with Evil and our days benight—
Unnatural things that lie *this side The Veil!*

The Collection
(a dramatic monologue)

"You are one of the very few to see my prize
Special collection. For only a dozen eyes
Save mine have beheld this sanctum, this secret room.
So very few have been bold enough to presume
To ask of my arcane grimoire library.

   But, as Fate would have it, you are very
Welcome to enter here. The lot is small,
Containing, of course, the well-known tomes: all
Of the "standard" titles (that you must surely know),
But here, in the center of the topmost row,
Are books long-hidden, texts that are unique!

   This one, for example, set down in Ancient Greek
And Hebrew—with some hieroglyphic Egyptian—
Fits, I believe, the kind of tome your description
Suggests. It is, of all these, that long-lost book:
Most rare, most eldritch…most unholy! Have a look
At the binding. It is leather *of the rarest skin.*
And there are heinous, fell secrets held within—
Words on grim vellum writ in human blood
And illustrations that can be understood
By very few. This finely illuminated
Leaf shows an avenging Golem being created.
On this page the dead god Osiris is revived,
Brought back! Those not-to-be-uttered words survived!
This tome the ages-hid, forbidden spells imparts
To the one who is Master of the damned Demonic Arts.

   I see full well your eagerness to peruse
This and my other rarities. But you confuse
My motives—just why I brought you here.

   What? Do I detect the first faint signs of fear?
In truth, only six before you have been told
That I've found the secret for never growing old!
Unfortunately for you, the spell requires
A human sacrifice. The very fires
Of Hell are needed. And—it surely seems—much pain!
But, blessing of sorts, you'll likely go insane
Before the essence of your soul is freed
To let me live another century. My need
Keeps me from caring whether it be sin
To use you thus. Well then…let us begin."

Khayyám's Rubáiyát

An Addendum for the Second Edition

**Rendered into English Verse
by Frank Coffman
from the prose translation
by Justin Huntly McCarthy**

Khayyám's Rubáiyát
Dedication to the Second Edition

These for thee, Omar, and thy worthy tribe,
Rendered by yet another humble scribe,
One who has drunken deeply of thy words
And wisdom—and most eagerly did imbibe.

A thousand years and more have moved along,
And still repolished are thy gems of song.
These but another spinning of thy themes
By one who has dared to seek to join the throng.

So, once again, these quatrains are recast
In homage—as were those from poets past
Who sought to catch the essence of thy soul,
Thou Inebriate of Life and Secrets Vast.

Cup-bearer, bring the flagon round and pour
The vine's blood into our cups once more.
Let the harps play, and let us sing along
On the lush grass beside those we adore—

Knowing the clay from which these cups are cast
Was once the dust of kings and beggars past;
The wine grown from fond youths and maidens fair,
Returned to earth to swell a number vast.

The nightbird sings in moonlit gardens. Those
Where the last petals cling unto the rose,
Where flagons empty and the singers close
Their song. Where Time—now with us—swiftly goes.

VIIIb
When I am dead, over my body lave
Ancient vintage. The same upon my grave.
And, should you want me at a later time,
Scrape dust before the tavern door to save.

XIVb
I passed a potter kneading the cold clay
And saw what he saw not—there on display:
My father's dust was in that wetted earth
That in the potter's hands, now lifeless, lay.

XVc
Man is a flagon and his soul the wine
He is a flute, his soul—tunes vile or fine.
O curious Khayyam, what then is a Man?
A lantern with a candle placed within.

XVIIIb
Khayyam, quit fretting for your sin's excess!
Don't plague your thoughts. Don't dampen happiness.
Because of Sinning was Fair Mercy made.
Those without Sin can't taste of sweet Forgiveness.

XXXb
When our blood beats quickest in this earthly run,
When quickly through the sky race the Steeds of the Sun,
I love to wander wide with lovely girls,
Making most merry—before earth hides that sun.

XXXVIIb
Give me my wine cup, for my heart's aflame!
Life slips like quicksilver back to whence it came.
Arise! Our fortune now's but a cheating dream.
Youth gushes past—a swift, but slowing, stream.

XLIIb
When I my fill of rich red wine have drunk,
And to the bliss of drunkenness have sunk—
A hundred miracles become then clear to me!
Vast mysteries to crystal clarity shrunk.

XLIIIb
Each day from Dawn to Dusk swift minutes pass—
As the swift sands through the upturned glass.
They won't return. The World to ruin runs.
Though helped by wine and mirth, so we—Alas!

LIVb
O my sad soul, pierced to the quick by sorrow,
When troubles sure will follow me tomorrow,
Why would you make a dwelling in this flesh
That has so little time on earth to borrow?

LVIII
Just as this wine takes on whatever shape
'Tis poured into, the essence of the grape—
Though quaffed—is not destroyed! Just so all Truths
Stay True—e'en though their Shadows may escape.

176

LXII
In mosque, in church, in synagogue, many more
Folk fear for Hell, hope for Heaven beyond the Door.
No such uncertainty to those who penetrate
To Deep Truth and the Secrets of the Wise explore.

LXIVb [A17]
Give up the search for things we can't attain.
Give in to the present joys that yet remain:
To touch long, beauteous tresses of your hair,
Like harp strings trembling in melodious strain.

LXVIIb [Bodleian MS. Attribured to Khayyam]
A sage came to me in a dream. "Asleep?"
He asked. "It is a lesser form of Death—so deep
That no true rose of joy will blossom there.
Rise and drink. There will be time enough for sleep."

LXXVb
Long, long before you or I were born
The cycles were set, spinning dusk and morn.
Be careful how we tread upon this dust—
Once the quick bodies by our forebears worn.

LXXVIIb
The Past, the Future—do not contemplate
Don't ponder what shall happen soon or late.
Live in each present moment of your life:
Think each a prize you've stolen from stark Fate.

LXXVIII
The peoples of Earth's many faiths have trod
Its many temple floors—wood, stone, or sod.
Their hymns and chants and prayers all rise unto,
Their symbols homage to the selfsame God.

LXXXI
Of all those Travellers who have passed *The Veil*,
Not one has e'er returned to tell the tale.
Rewarded is the man of humble heart,
Sincere and contrite. Mere prayer does not avail.

LXXXVIII
True: some are bound for Heaven, some for Hell.
I have a thirst that no sweet wine can quell.
I behold a Place that I cannot describe;
I hold a Secret that I cannot tell.

XCVIIb
Between sober and drunk there is a place:
When sober, of happiness there is no trace;
When drunk, a state of blessed ignorance prevails.
Somewhere between the two I find Life's face.

XCIX
Do not give yourself up to passion's raging fire,
Or surrender to insatiable desire.
Seek, rather, whence you came and whither go;
To learn just who you are you should aspire.

Cb

Who would create a cup and later dream
Of crushing it? It is a strange extreme.
Yet all these lovely bodies, faces, limbs
Will be so crushed. The Maker will redeem.

CIVb

O, all my friends, gather when I am sped,
And, at that meeting, do not mourn me dead.
When the cup-bearer brings round the flagon full,
Drink to Old Khayyám and the life he led.

CVIII

The Wise will seek Contentment of the Heart—
Either through devotion that God may Grace impart,
Or Soul's Tranquility through the brimming cup—
Each path may reach that Goal. Aye! That's the Art.

CXIII

At one time I drew close to prayer and fast,
But such devotions—Alas!—were not to last.
E'en a half measure of the sweet, red wine
Has made my short-lived zeal a thing of the past.

CXXVI

Pray, Master, make lawful but one of our desires:
Whether the love of the grape or passion's fires.
We would walk strait such a clear path to You—
Yet You see and frown on all that here transpires.

CXXXIV
Put Wisdom by and take the Cup in hand;
Cease now of Heaven or Hell to understand.
Yea! Sell thy silken turban and with the price
Buy wine! For thee a woolen cap is grand.

CXLIII
On my last night upon this troubled Earth,
I will clamor for sweet wine and passion's mirth.
I shall think not of Heaven nor of Hell,
But love and wine will put off this world's dearth.

CLXIV
Know that thy fleshly body is of naught,
Know that the Seven Heaven's can't be bought.
Know thou delight in this Kingdom of Misrule.
Know brief life as a fleeting moment caught.

CLXXIV
Our days abiding here are of no worth
Without the sweet red wine and blissful mirth
We may share with she who bears the brimming cup
Or plays the lute—Joy! Pleasure! while on earth.

CLXXV
Drawn along by the flying feet of Time,
My life is overwhelmed. It is a crime
Gifts given the undeserving, but, in Life's Garden,
My heart's a closed rosebud, a bloody tulip in my prime.

CLXXIX

Get yourself dancing girls, wine, a mistress fair;
Seek a meadow, limpid stream agushing there.
Vex yourself not with thoughts of some dark Hell.
Those gifts: the only Heaven of which I'm aware.

CLXXXI

Don't think the "call of duty" has called me here
To the mosque—or to lift up my voice in prayer.
One day I stole a prayer rug—my carpet was worn.
Ever since, I return when my old one's in disrepair.

CXCVII

Sweet wine gives wings to those of heavy heart;
On the cheek of Wisdom, wine is the beauty mark's art.
I've briefly foregone it—but Ramadan has fled.
So back to the wine! I plan to drink my part!

CCVIII

May the tavern always hold a reveling throng!
May the pains of the "saintly" grow! That can't be wrong.
May their robes fall in rags, their blue gowns trampled
Underfoot by the topers, their crying loud and long!

CCXI

How long with dyes and colors will you be vain?
How long vexed by thought of Good or Bad remain?
Were you the Fountain of Youth, the Water of Life,
You will end in the bosom of Earth—that much is plain.

CCXVI

How long in this world's furnace will we be consumed?
Arise! Cast off all sadness! We are not entombed
Yet. Today, at least, is a day we should rejoice!
Come! Let rosy wine drinking be resumed!

CCXVII

I sometimes battle my passions—this is true.
My past iniquities I can't undo.
I must trust in Your Mercy, despite my many sins,
Knowing full well that none are hidden from You.

CCXXVI

O Thou, all seek Thee—yet in great despair
Both dervish and rich man know that Thou art there.
All eyes might see Thee, yet all eyes are blind.
Thy name is in all mouths, yet none can hear.

CCXLIV

Since Your sweet Mercy is vouchsafed to me,
I have no fear for my every iniquity.
The Leaves of the Book give me no cause for terror.
And I can smile for your dear clemency.

CCL

Though my members will scatter like leaves before the wind,
I will rejoice when I come to this Life's End.
My spirit shall be sifted through a Great Sieve,
This world's Builder shall prove my final Friend.

CCLXIII

Sometimes the draught of our life is crystal clear;
Sometimes clouded; sometime our robes of dear
Finest silk; sometimes of rougher wool.
These we abide. But what when Death is near?

CCLXIV

The greatest wisdom and the heart's delight
Come from the flagon of wine sweet and bright.
Dwell not upon your time upon this earth.
Wherein the soul, imprisoned, is held tight.

CCLXVI

No man has pierced the Secret of The Cause,
Nor stepped outside himself. Our nature's laws
Are understood by neither pupil nor master.
Imperfect we are—with universal flaws.

CCLXIX

They say, "When the moon of Ramadan is in the sky,
One must foreswear the bliss of wine." But I
Propose—when the required festival is done—
To become sodden, drink up my whole supply!

CCLXXVI

How long will you remain in love with Life,
Or search for the Source of Being? All is strife.
Drink wine! Since all lives are leading but to death,
Sleep or be drunk—for with sorrows our lives are rife.

CCLXXXIV
No one has drawn aside Fate's tenebrous Veil.
All seeking Divine Knowledge are doomed to fail.
Over seventy years of thought, both day and night,
I've sought to solve these enigmas—to no avail.

CCLXXXV
Drink not thy wine in the company of fools,
Those with no wit, no sense of manners' rules.
While drinking you will suffer from their folly,
When morning comes, the idiot pukes and drools.

CCXCVIII
Happy the heart who goes through this world unknown,
Whose hypocrisies to this world are never shown,
Who, like the sage, is translated to the skies,
Not adding to Mankind's universal groan.

CCCVIII
How long will you chide us, foolish devotee?
Scorn we frequenters of the tavern—plain to see?
With cup in hand and loved one by our side,
We scorn your path, your vile hypocrisy.

CCCXXI
A plague upon hypocrisy! O cub-bearer, I'm content
Come hither with the wine! I shan't repent.
I'll sell my prayer cloth and my sacred turban,
And buy more wine with money so well spent.

CCCXXV

O heart, my heart, you will never know the Why?
Or know more than the Wise. Oh no, not I.
I'll make for myself a heaven here with wine,
Never knowing whither—afterwards—I fly.

CCCXXVIII

O cub-bearer, we are but earth, so tune the lute.
That we are soft as air there's no dispute.
To understand one, as hard as one hundred thousand!
Bring wine! The glorious essence of the fruit.

CCCXXXI

We have the wine, the well-beloved, the morning.
How long will tales of old be told? A warning
Lingers still. Bring the sweet peace of soul,
For these stop-griefs may leave or die aborning.

CCCXXXII

When, at my pleasure, wine my reason grips,
And my poor hermit heart from wisdom slips,
Do not in this bleak pilgrimage deny the cup;
Keep fast the delights of wine and lover's lips.

CCCXXXVI

Arise! Dash down your cares and let them burn.
Along life's road, no matter how you yearn
For the fortune of others, their share of merriment.
You only have one chance—so take your turn.

CCCXLII
Thou hast stamped us with a seal most strange,
Allowed us deeds we cannot rearrange.
Forsooth, it was Thee who drew me from the Void.
How can I—thus created—hope to change?

CCCXLVIb
Now You are hidden and Your Face not shown;
Now You are seen in all Creation known.
For Your own delight all Wonders You perform—
Being at once the Player and the Dice You've thrown.

CCCLVII
O Saki, bring the cup of delightful wine.
It is for us the juice most near Divine.
It is like a chain linking in servitude
Both fools and sages. Sweet captivity mine!

CCCLX
Last night, at tavern, my old friend bade me take
A cup. But I his offer did forsake.
"I'll drink no more," I said. But he replied,
"Drink my good friend. Drink for our friendship's sake."

CCCLXII
Heed not the speech of women frivolous,
But seize the cup of wine from the beauteous.
All who have trod this earth, yea one by one
Have vanished—and not one returned to us.

CCCLXIV

At that palace that reached up to the heavens above,
'Fore which now-dead kings have bowed, we stood in love
And heard, from those battlements that touched the clouds,
The soft coo-coo-ing of the ringnecked dove.

CCCLXIX

The strong wine of our being may be exalted,
When we, once lowly, from this earth are vaulted.
When we are free of flesh's fierce dominion,
We return to earth who bore us—no longer faulted.

CCCLXXV

Be kind to revellers of Old Khayyám's kind.
There is one secret that you best should mind:
Away with prayers and fasting! Drink you deep
The sweet red wine—and leave your cares behind.

CCCXCIV

Since it seems you know the secrets, though a youth,
Why so racked with doubts and despair? The Truth
Is that Life's Wheel turns not for your pleasure.
Be merry while you still draw breath—Forsooth!

CCCXCVII

Thanks to the cup, O Saki, my breath remains.
But, in this Creation, discontent remains.
Of yestere'en's wine, only one flagon's left.
And I know not how much of my life remains.

CCCCII
A mouthful of wine is better than any empire!
'Tis better than Feridoun's kingdom to acquire.
The stopper in the flagon's beckoning lips—
More precious than Kai-Khosrou's crown of jeweled fire.

CCCCV
O Thou that turnest day and night to lust,
Think'st not upon The Heavy Day? 'Tis just
Thou shouldst look to thyself—to thy last breath—
To the End thou sharest with all, as sure thou must.

CCCCIX
In the scheme of existence we are the keys,
We have the essence of the Divine. Wise eyes
See this. The hoop of the world is like a ring,
And we the fine-worked gems on that great prize.

CCCCXIII
O friend, grieve not how your time on earth's been spent,
Be tranquil in your days. Do not repent.
It matters little what you've done or said
Or how you're stained in the span that you've been lent.

CCCCXVI
Arise, O cup-bearer, from thy place of sleep.
Give us clear wine, and let us drink full deep.
Too soon the cups of our skulls will flagons be.
They hold now rarest spirits that will not keep.

CCCCXXIV
Fashioned by Thy power I've lived a life in grace.
Would I could live another span in disgrace,
That I might see the greater: Thy power of Pity—
Or my great faults no Pity should erase.

CCCCXXXVIII
Heaven above is but an inverted bowl.
And cup and jar are helpmates to the soul.
So press your lips upon the cup's sweet lips
And share the blood of life. Now there's a goal!

To be Incorporated into the Second Edition—
adding 72 ruba'i to the First Edition's 327
for a total of 399 quatrains
selected and rendered into English Verse
from Justin Huntly McCarthy's
466 translations of the ruba'i into English Prose

Tamam Shud
[The Very End]

GLOSSARY OF FORMS

Corrigenda

In both of my first two collections, *The Coven's Hornbook & Other Poems* and *Black Flames & Gleaming Shadows,* I've listed my "invented" forms of "Coffman Sonnet, Type 1" and "Coffman Sonnet, Type 2" in error. I cannot claim "prior" or even "simultaneous" invention for either of the forms, I so named, for I have discovered that both of these rhyme schemes were invented and used prior to my "naming" them. I *will* claim "independent invention."

To give credit where credit is due; however, the form I called "Coffman Sonnet, Type 1" [rhyme scheme: [abccba deffed gg] is actually a "Scupham Sonnet," a form invented and used by the fine British poet, Peter Scupham.

The sonnet I dubbed "Coffman Sonnet, Type 2" [with rhyme scheme: abcabc defdef gg] is actually a "Brisbane Sonnet," invented by Laurence Eberhart, founder and moderator of the *Every Sonnet* blog—which is a great service to all verse poets and especially to sonneteers.

My apologies to both of these fine poets for erroneously appropriating their sonnet schemes by mis-naming them. I have subsequently come up with more sonnet varieties that, I believe, are unique inventions—and my own.

Rather than shuffle the original Type 3 and Type 4 that I identified in my first two collections, I have come up with "replacement" #s 1 and 2— and added a few more [see below in the item: COFFMAN SONNETS which lists and subdivides the various forms by type and number and explains the basic pattern/schemes.

See also the entry on MEGASONNETS, since I have invented four 21-line forms that are based on the mathmatical expansion of the traditional sonnet's 14 lines, inspired by the mathmatical reduction done by G. M. Hopkins with his "Curtal Sonnet."

Awdl Gywydd [pronounced "ow-dull ge-outh"] is one of the 24 official Welsh meters. It is done in quatrains of seven-syllable lines (heptasyllabic). The final syllable of the first and third lines of each quatrain should cross-rhyme into a middle syllable (3, 4, or 5) of the next line (into lines 2 and 4, respectively). The second and fourth lines end rhyme. I added two lines following three such quatrains to creat the **Awdl Gywydd Sonnet.***

BALASSI STANZA AND BALASSI SONNET* The Balassi Stanza was the inspiration for my conversion of the form into a sonnet. It is attributed to Bálint Balassi (1554-1594) who is probably Hungary's best known Renaissance poet. He transformed it from a three-line form consisting of 19-syllable lines with internal rhymes into three-line groups of 6-6-and 7 syllables, with the six-syllable lines ending with what would be the "internal" rhyme of the long 19-syllable version and the seven-syllable line carrying the main rhyme, thus: aabccbddb for a nonain stanza or poem.

I have reverted a bit toward the older form in my Ballassi Stanza Sonnet* by using divisions of 12-7 and providing the internal rhymes in the twelve-syllable lines with the rhyme on syllables 6 and 12. Thus, the expansion of Balassi's pattern into an octave of 12-7-12-7-12-7-12-7 with the shorter lines carrying the main rhyme, followed by a sestet of 12-7-12-7-12-7—again with the internal rhymes different and the shorter lines carrying the main rhyme, but also on a different rhyme from the octave.

BALLADE SUPREME A DOUBLE REFRAIN is a variant of the Ballade with more lines than the normal Ballade, and, as the name indicates, two refrain phrases or lines at work. It is isosyllabic [written in syllable-count/syllabic meter with any regularized syllable count]. The poem is 35 lines long, divided into three ten line verses and a five-line *envoi*. Usually the syllable count per line is 8 or 10. It has two refrains.

The rhyming and repeating structure are thus: ababbCcdcD / ababbCcdcD / ababbCcdcD / cCdcD. The C and D represent the two refrains.

BRETON COUPLETS date from the 14th century A.D. and are octosyllabic rhymed couplets, ideally with internal rhyme on the 4th and 7th syllables. **THE BRETON COUPLET SONNET*** uses seven of these couplets to make 14 lines.

BYR A THODDAID [SONNET*](bur a tothaid): This Welsh measure combines an eight-syllable couplet with another type of couplet called *Toddaid Byr*. **TODDAID BYR** consists of ten syllables, followed by six. *In the ten-syllable line the main rhyme is found before the end, and the syllables that follow that main rhyme must be linked—by rhyme, alliteration, or assonance—with the early syllables in the six-syllable line.*

192

Dark is this maze wherein I err.
No Theseus I; no comforter,
No Ariadne at my SIDE, to HOLD
Her GOLDen skein as GUIDE.
      —Rolfe Humphries, "The Labyrinth"
      from *Green Armor on Green Ground* (my emphases)

I added a couplet to three quatrains of Byr a Thoddaid to make a 14-line sonnet.

CANOPUS is an invented verse form which stresses a "continuous flow of thought". This is attributed to author Clement Wood of *The Complete Rhyming Dictionary and Poet's Craft* [1936]. The Canopus is a seven-syllable stanza or poem (a heptastich) written in iambic pentameter. Its rhyme scheme is ababcbc. Hence, my **CANOPUS SONNET*** uses two Canopus stanzas to make 14 lines for the sonnet and rhymes **ababcba dedefef**.

CAUDATE ["TAILED"] SONNET (MILTONIC) is a sonnet in the Italian/Petrarchan form with an added "tail" [Latin: *caudus*] of varied meter from the body of the poem. The rhyme scheme is: abbaabba ‖ cdecde ‖ EffFgg where the E and F are in iambic trimeter the f's and g's pentameter.

CHUEH-CHU (Chinese for "sonnet cut short" as used by Li Po and Tu Fu): The Chueh-Chu consists of 8 lines rhyming **abcbdbeb** I have made a fourteener for the **CHUEH-CHU SONNET*** by repeating the pattern of the first six after the 8 **abcbdbeb ‖ fghgig**. The **CH'I-YEN-SHIH METER** dictates Heptasyllabic lines with ALL monosyllable words and a caesura after the fourth word in each line. I have sought to follow this pattern.

CLOGYRNACH is a Welsh form in syllabic meter (as are all the Welsh, and indeed, all the Celtic language meters). It is written in six-line stanzas (hexastiches/hexains) rhyming **aabbba** with varying line lengths of 8-8-5-5-3-3 syllables. I have also incorporated some of **the Welsh "Harmonies,"** called Cynghanedd (q.v.), and have added two lines following two clogyrnachs to make a **CLOGYRNACH SONNET***.

Coffman Sonnets (explanation of invented types)

Type 1 [new] (see *corrigenda* above): Rhyme Scheme of **abbacddceffegg** (also called a "Hybrid Sonnet" at EverySonnet blog).

Type 2 [new] (see *corregenda* above): Based upon a 4-6-4 pattern of lines. Three variant forms according to this division: The Italian Variation (2I): **abba cdeedc fggh**; The English Variation (2E): **abab cdecde fgfg**; and ANY COMBINATION of the two quatrain types [**xyyx or xyxy**] or septets [**xyzzyx or xyzxyz**]—would be (2V) for "variant."

Type 3: Based upon a division of lines into 5-5-4 (two pentains and a quatrain) and rhyming: **abcba deced** with a final quatrain of ANY of the following: **fggf, fgfg,** or **ffgg**.

Type 4: Based upon a division of lines into 4-5-5. The rhyme pattern would be: an opening quatrain in any of the following rhyme patterns: **abba, abab,** or **aabb** followed by **cdcdc efefe**.

Type 5: An octave/sestet form with an abnormal/reflexive second quatrain in the Italian Octave (**abbabaab**, rather than **abbaabba**). There are four variants, based upon the scheme used in the Sestet: **cdcdee** (5E, "English"); **cddcee** (5W, "Wyatt's Ending"); and two (5I, "Italian": **cdecde** or **cdcdcd**).

Type 6: abbacddcefefgg.

Cornish Hexains: Are hexaines (six-line stanzas) of any length from 4 to 9 syllables The rhyme sceme is **aabccb**. I've added a couplet to make the sonnet.

Curtal Sonnet: A form invented by Fr. Gerard Manley Hopkins based upon a mathmatical reduction of the Italian/Petrarchan sonnet's octave and sestet structure. The ratio of 8:6 may be reduced to 6:4.5 which is exactly what Hopkins did in his "curtail [curtailed] sonnets." Perhaps the more famous is "Pied Beauty":

> Glory be to God for dappled things –
>   For skies of couple-colour as a brinded cow;
>   For rose-moles all in stipple upon trout that swim;
> Fresh-firecoal chestnut-falls; finches' wings;
>   Landscape plotted and pieced – fold, fallow, and plough;
>   And áll trádes, their gear and tackle and trim.

194

All things counter, original, spare, strange;
   Whatever is fickle, freckled (who knows how?)
   With swift, slow; sweet, sour; adazzle, dim;
He fathers-forth whose beauty is past change:
   Praise him.

CYNGHANEDD: The Welsh poets use four basic types of **CYNGHANEDD** (king-a-neth) "Harmonies" that may appear in any of their 24 Official Meters. They are, essentially, special types of echoing, alliteration, assonance, consonance, and internal rhyme used to enhance the musical quality of the verses. **NOTE:** The following explanations are derived from poet Rolfe Humphries excellent book of Welsh meters in English, *Green Armor on Green Ground*. They are also somewhat simplified in explanation, not taking into account certain rules for rising or falling meters and other echo restrictions. They are all challenging in English. The four types are:

CYNDHANEDD DRAWS (drowse): in which alliteration is required only in the beginning portion and the ending portion of a line, the middle portion being bypassed—"a **c**at may look at a **k**ing" or "he **r**ode to the city of **R**ome."

CYNHANEDD GROES (gro-ess): in which the consonants of the first half of a line are repeated in the same order in the second half of the line with alliteration or even double-deep alliteration (on two sounds)—an English example is "**on** a **s**ettee **in** a **c**ity"—a Welsh example is "**Cr**upl y **c**ur, **cr**oyw e**pil c**of" [note that *final consonants in the halves do not need to alliterate* only initial sets—usually two in number.

CYNGHANEDD LUSG (lusg): The last syllable of a word in the early part of the line must rhyme with the next-to-last syllable of the line which must be a word of 2 or 3 syllables with its accent on the rhymed penultimate syllable "Be**gin** to sing in **Win**ter."

CYNGHANEDD SAIN (sen): To my mind the most interesting, although difficult of these various harmonies. A challenge, but a great musical effect when achieved. The line contains an internal rhyme prior to its end, and the second of the rhymed words must alliterate—but not rhyme— with the last word of the line (one of mine):

   "He **y**ear**n**ed to **learn** the secrets that were **l**ost.
   Over eldritch **l**ore he had **p**oured: chants, **p**oems,
   Thirs**t**ing for the ac**curst**. Bought at great **c**ost."
         —from "The Summoner"

Cywydd Deuair Hirion (cowith doayr hiryon): is a seven-syllable couplet that "light rhyme" in that one of the lines ends on an accented syllable while the other ends on an unaccented syllable. Examples: sand:England, dead:infested. A poem using seven such couplets would be a **Cywydd Deuair Hirion Sonnet***. Note also, that such poems are usually heavy in Cynghanedd (q.v.).

Daina [Sonnet]: The Daina is a Latvian form of octosyllabic quatrains using no end rhymes (although rare rhymes or alliterations may occur). I added two lines to three Daina to make the **Daina Sonnet.***

Dantean Canzone Sonnet*: The canzone resembles a sonnet but, while the sonnet is fixed at 14 lines, a canzone stanza can range from seven to 20 lines. Furthermore, a canzone runs from one to seven stanzas, and has a variety of rhyme schemes. Most canzone lines contain 10 or 11 syllables, but these too can vary. Because the canzone is not as fixed as a sonnet, it is often easier to write.

The canzone has no standard rhyme scheme, but I have chosen the pattern from a short, single-stanza canzone—coincidentally 14 lines—that of Dante's "Canzone 1" from *La Vita Nuovo*.

Decima italiana [Sonnet]: As the name of the form indicates, the Decima Italiana is an Italian form with 10 lines. The poem uses eight syllable lines with a rhyme scheme of ababc dedec. C-words must be accented/stressed and first D-line must begin a new sentence Add in a rhymed quatrain to make the sonnet. I've used fcfc to keep the ending c rhyme of the two pentains [and, also, to use my initials FC :-)]

Dolnik: The Dolnik is a Russion form using octosyllabic lines, blending anapests and iambs: uu/u/uu/ or uu/uu/u/. Additional syllables may follow the eighth, but the the eighth always carries the rhyme: ababbcbc, but *it can be set in quatrains of abcb* (ballad-like). For the Dolnik Sonnet,* the pattern of abab bcbc dedede works. In my example, I've used abcb cded afcfef although final edfdff makes more interlocking sense. Often much alliteration is used in the Dolnik.

196

DRÓTTKVÆTT: The Dróttkvætt (short for Dróttkvætt Háttr)

The meter used by the Drótt, the retainers of the king, the staple meter of skaldic poetry is an Old Norse-Icelandic form done in eight line stanzas (octostiches/octaves) with each line being six syllables long. Each line (or segment, if presented in longer lines of 12 syllables) has, ideally, three accented and three unaccented syllables. Most lines end in a trochee, often a two-syllable feminine ending (/u). Every two six-syllable lines or segments (half lines) are bound by alliteration, which MUST fall on the first stressed syllable of the second line—following at least two alliterations on that sound in the first line. As with many Old Norse-Icelandic and Germanic forms in general, there is often heavy use of internal rhyme, full rhyme on the even numbered lines [in other words, final sounds of longer lines if two six-syllable segments are joined], often slant rhyming or assonance on the odd numbered lines. Germanic "kennings" (word compound metaphors like "Oden's Door" for a "Shield" or "Sky Candle" for "Sun."

This is the standard meter for the early ON poems in — DRAPA

Later ON poems use **HYRNHENT /HYRNHENDA** – same, but with 8-syllable lines.

Also another variant (according to Snorri Sturlussen in his *Skaldskaparmal [The Poesy of the Skalds]*) is **DRAUGHENT**, the same using 7-syllable lines with the accent in the second line of each pair as the extra-metrical.

DRUTAVILAMBITA METER (SANSKRIT): Is written in duodecaslyllabic lines (12-syllables per line) and composed in the strict measure consisting of a fourth paeon, two anapests, and an iamb: uuu/uu/uu/u/. Originally, and in Sanskrit, it is a Quantitative Meter (based on "Long" or "Short" syllables, rather than the Qualitative (Accent-Counting) meters of modern English and other European languages. The scansion above is only an approximation of the flow of **DRUTAVILAMBITA** ("Long, then Short"). But, since it is a "Rising Meter," with unstressed syllables building "UP" to the stressed syllables, it can fit nicely into English, where the iambic rhythm is natural. Rhyme is allowable, but not necessary. For my epyllion, *The Decipherment*, I have chosen to use primarily blank verse with this meter.

I have also used the scanning method of three levels of accent, and have chosen to consider either unstressed or light stressed (levels 1 and 2 as is usually used to indicate this [or U for unstressed and \ for mild stress])

and only considered full or dominant stress (level 3 or /) as accented. This allowed more freedom, especially in the first "foot" of the line, the fourth paeon [uuu/]. Four-syllable feet are not normally used in English—even in variation.

Englyn Cyrch: Englyn Cyrch (en-glin circh "two rhyme englyn"), one of the 24 Official Welsh Meters—an *Englyn* "verse" that employs *Cyrch* ("internal rhyme"). It is written in any number of heptasyllabic quatrains made up of two *Cywydd* (ki-with) couplets, the first being a *Cywydd Deu-air Hirion* (ki-with dyawr hiryon) and the second being an *Awdl Gywydd* (audel giwith). Rhyme is AaBA with the first couplet light-rhyming with a masculine (stressed ending) in line one and a feminine (unstressed syllable ending) in line 2, and the B rhyme of the end of line 3 cross-rhyming into the middle of line 4. The pattern is:
x x x x x x A (stressed last syllable)
x x x x x Xa (unstressed last syllable)
x x x x x x B
x[B x x]xxA (B) can be the 2nd, 3rd, or 4th syllable of the fourth line.
My **Englyn Cyrch-Terza Rima Sonnet***, leaves out the second line of the englyn quatrains, creating the **aba bcb**, etc. interlocking pattern of Terza Rima, but keeping the cross-rhymes and the essential line lengths. The full Engly Cyrch quatrains could be used to do an Interlocking Englyn Cyrch-Rhubaiyat sonnet: **aaba bbcb ccdc dd** with the concluding couplet being simply a rhymed heptasyllabic couplet.

Espinela [Sonnet*]: The Espinela is a Spanish form named for the poet Vicente Gómez Martínez-Espinel (1550-1624). It consists of 10 octosyllabic lines with a break after the fourth. The rhyme scheme is **abba || accddc**. To make an **Espnela Sonnet*** I added an extra quatrain to have 14 lines.

Ghazal [Ghazal Sonnet*] The Ghazal is an Arabic form composed in couplets and distiches (two-line stanzas). The first two-line stanza is a true couplet with the *refrain* rhymed word or short phrase ending both of the first two lines. Following that, in each two-line group the refrain word or phrase must end the second line. Often, following the initial couplet, a rhyme is carried through all of the second lines *appearing immediately prior to the refrain*. I have done this in the seven distiches of my sonnet.

GWAWDODYN [GWAWDODYN SONNET*]: [Welsh Meter] The Gwawdodyn (gwow-dodin) is a four line stanza on 9-9-10-9 syllable counts and rhymed **aaba**. The B-word may rhyme with a B-word internally in the same line, OR, if the rhyme sound is prior to the final syllable, it cross-rhymes into the middle of the fourth line. I have done the **GWAWDODYN SONNET*** by adding a nonosyllabic couplet after three Gwawdodyns.

HEXAMETER: The most important Classical metre (also called the "Heroic Hexamter" or the "Epic Hexameter," used by Homer and Virgil both (as well as in Horace's satires and Ovid's *Metamorphoses*). It was supposedly invented by the god Hermes. The classical hexameters are lines of six feet, the feet in the line arranged thus:
A dactylic hexameter has six feet, as the name denotes. In strict dactylic hexameter, each foot would be a dactyl (a long and two short syllables OR /uu in accentual-syllabic scansion), but classical meter allows for the substitution of a spondee (two long [or accented] syllables, //) in place of a dactyl *in most positions*. Specifically, the first four feet can either be dactyls or spondees more or less freely. The fifth foot is usually a dactyl (around 95% of the time in Homer).
The sixth foot can be filled by either a trochee (a long then short syllable, or /u) or a spondee (//). Thus the dactylic line most normally is scanned as follows: /uu/uu/uu/uu/uu/u (with the frequent spondee substitutions (usually no more than two per line, most often only one). Longfellow's demonstration of it in *Evangeline* is a good approximation of the sound:

"This is the forest primeval. The murmuring pines and the hemlocks,
Bearded with moss, and in garments green, indistinct in the twilight,
Stand like Druids of eld, with voices sad and prophetic,
Stand like harpers hoar, with beards that rest on their bosoms...."

ILLINI SONNET: The Illini Sonnet is an invented form that I discovered in Viola Berg's book, *Pathways for the Poet* [1977]. It is credited as the invention of Nel Modglin and is likely named for the Native American tribe or, more likely, for the name of athletic teams at the University of Illinois, her alma mater (also mine). The rhyme scheme is **abcabcdbcdecce**, but the more unusual aspect is the variating line lengths. Lines 1, 4, 5, 8, 9, and 12 are iambic tetrameter and the others are the normal pentameter.

KASA [KOREAN] AND KASA SONNET* The Kasa is written in eight-syllable lines. Each line, ideally, divides into two four-syllable parts or phrases. The poem does not end rhyme, but, rather, it *Head-Rhymes with the first words of lines finding an echo in rhyme with at least one other line of the poem. It must at the very least consonate with another line.* The Kasa Sonnet is simply fourteen lines in this mode.

MEGASONNETS: My invented forms of the "Megasonnet" are based upon the same mathmatics that Gerard Manley Hopkins used to create his "Curtal" [curtailed] Sonnet. Where Hopkins used the proportions of the Italian Sonnet, octave and sestet: 8:6, the "Megasonnet" is an expansion of the basic sonnet from 14 lines to 21 lines. This I have done with four types of traditional sonnets.

First, the ITALIAN MEGASONNET is, of course, based upon the traditional Italian (Petrarchan) Sonnet with actual octave and sestet arrangement. But, instead of 8:6 in the pattern of the Italian Octave (**abbaabba**) and sestet (usually **cdcdcd** or **cdecde**, but any combination, so long as the poem *DOES NOT* end in a couplet—I have set the following 12-9 proportions (a simply mathmatical expansion of the 8:6 ratio). The rhyme scheme is as follows: **abccbaabccba defdefdef**.

Second, the ENGLISH MEGASONNET is based upon the traditional English (Shakespearean) Sonnet with the rhyme scheme [actually invented by Henry Howard, Earl of Surrey] of: **abab cdcd efef gg**. Again, I have simply expanded this to: **abcabc defdef ghighi jjj** OR **jxj** where "x" is either g, h, or i—this so as not to confine the poet to a necessary triplet; although ideal for the form, but successful triplets are sometimes difficult to find, and the repeat of a rhyme from the last sestet provides a nice echo.

Third, the SPENSERIAN MEGASONNET, based upon the Spenserian Sonnet in which Spenser "re-comlicated" the English Sonnet by interlocking the quatrains: **abab bcbc cdcd ee** (thus making it as difficult to rhyme as the Italian form) I have expanded into: **abcabc bcdbcd cdecde fff** or **f [c, d, or e] f.**

Fourth, and finally [but which could and, perhaps, should have been first, is the **LENTINIAN [SICILLIAN] MEGASONNET**, named for the first true sonnetteer and inventor of the form, developed from the eight-line form of the Strambotto, Giacomo de Lentino (as most scholars of the sonnet now contend). The earliest sonnets actually used the Sicilian Octave (**abababab**) rather than the Italian Octave [envelope] (**abbaabba**) seen in Petrarch, Dante, Michaelangelo and others—hence, the Italian Sonnet of tradition. Di Lentino's sonnet rhymed **abababab cdcdcd**. Thus the Lintinian-Sicillian Megasonnet rhymes: **abcabcabcabc defdefdef**.

MINNESANG (German "love song"): People who wrote and performed Minnesang were known as Minnesänger, and a single song was called a "Minnelied."

The Minnesang is written in octasyllabic quatrains of **abcb abcb** (usually two of them). I've added **ddefef** to make a **MINNESANG SONNET*** – still all in octosyllabic lines.

MUZARI METER [PERSIAN] is composed in couplets [*Mathnavi*] of 14- syllable lines. The normal line rhythm is //u /u/u u//u u/. This is a difficult meter to use with regularity in English. We can but try.

PROTO-WORLD GRAMMAR: Presupposes common ancestor for all of the world's languages, based upon the hypothesis of Monogenesis—that 100,000 to 200,000 years ago, a single, original human language (sometimes also called "Proto-Sapiens" was born and began splitting off into the many and various world language families.

In a 2011 paper, Murray Gell-Mann and Merritt Ruhlen argued that the ancestral language had *subject–object–verb* (*SOV*) word order. The reason for thinking so is that in the world's natural language families, it is typical for the original "proto-"language to have an SOV word order, though languages that evolve from them sometimes deviate. Their proposal develops an earlier one made by Talmy Givón (1979).

Languages with SOV word order have a strong tendency to have other word orders in common, such as:

- *Adjectives precede the nouns they modify.*
- *Dependent genitives precede the nouns they modify.*

201

PROTO-WORLD GRAMMAR (CONT.)

‹   *"Prepositions" are really "postpositions", following the nouns they refer to.*

For example, instead of saying The man goes to the wide river, as in English, Ruhlen's Proto-Human speakers would have said "Man wide river to goes." I have used this hypothesis in the writing of my **PROTO-WORLD SONNET***.

RIMAS DISSOLUTAS: was popular with 12th and 13th century French poets. It is a poem that rhymes, and yet, in a way, doesn't rhyme!? Each stanza contains no end rhymes, BUT each line in each stanza rhymes with the corresponding line in the next stanza—sometimes employing an envoi at the end making use of at least one more than half of the previously used rhyme sounds. There are no rules for meter, line length, or syllables—except that it should be consistent from stanza to stanza.

RUBÁI: The Rubái is a Persian quatrain pattern, rhymed **aaba**. A **RUBÁIYÁT** is a longer poem composed in Rubái. While they need not be, the quatrains of a Rubáiyát *may be interlocked, with the unrhymed line from one stanza being picked up as the primary rhyme in each subsequent stanza:* **aaba bbcb ccdc, etc.** This is an **INTERLOCKING RUBÁIYÁT**. The **RUBÁIYÁT SONNET*** rhymes: **aaba bbcb ccdc dd.** [same scheme if read backwards!]

SEPTILLA [SONNET*]: The Septilla or "Spanish Septet" is, of course, a seven-line stanza—thus, making it perfect for two of them to make a **SEPTILLA SONNET.*** There are two commen rhyme patterns: **aabccba** or **abbacca**. I have used both.

SESTINA SONNET [RHYMED]*: is my invented form, based upon the mathmatical pattern of arrangement of the Sestina, but limiting the poem to 14 lines. The Sestina Sonnet* need not rhyme, and the traditional Sestina use of same end words could be used. It breaks into two hexains and a couplet—with ALL of the word or rhyme repeats being used in the final two couplets (6 words or rhymes in each).

The pattern of the lines by numbers: 123456 615243 [364] [215]

My poem in rhymed lines: **abcabc || cabbac || [cca] [abb]**

Snam Suad (Irish): Snam Suad is an intricate and thickly rhymed Irish form. It is very demanding, and I have only rendered a close approximation of its rhyme and flow in English. The rules are complex, but it is based on eight three-syllable rhyming lines or segments—making for 24-syllable "stanzas." The rhyme scheme is **aabcdddc** which I have broken in twelve-syllable lines, thus creating rhymed couplets. Seven such "lines" make up the **Snam Suad Sonnet.***

Additional rules are: lines four and eight are 3-syllable words, all other lines end in monosyllabic words, lines two and three share consonance, lines three and four, six and seven, and four and seven share alliteration, line seven uses alliteration. I have NOT followed all of these special restrictions in my poem. The heavy rhyming is rigorous enough a test.

Sonnet [General Information]:

I have noted in many places elsewhere, and herein in my "Preface," that I consider myself primarily a "sonneteer." While certainly nearly all of my poetry is formalist and traditionalist in the use of meter and, in the vast majority of cases, rhyme, my mind seems to think "sonnet first" or "how do I make this ancient, medieval, exotic, or cross-cultural form into a sonnet?"

I believe the sonnet to be, not only the ubiquitous fixed form of Western Poesy, but also the "perfect poetic paragraph," the little square of ink upon the page, the true verse poet's test, the ideal task presented for concision/compactness/compression of thought, and for concentration of impact upon the reader or auditor. It also presents the constructional challenges of meter and rhyme (in most cases) to the poet, as well as—with some of its forms (such as the exacting schemes of the Italian, the Sicilian, or the Spenserian) traditions and rules that are quite exacting.

To extend and enhance those normal challenges, I usually begin by trying to "hybridize" any new form I encounter into a meld with the sonnet form in some way. Hence, the many and various sonnets in this book.

While there are some "purists" who insist that the "True Sonnet" MUST BE the Italian or Petrarchan model (based upon the more than 300 sonnets Francesco Petrarca wrote to his Platonic love interest—both during her life and following her early demise.

I disagree strongly with this premise on two major counts: first, the actual first sonnets were not penned by Petrarch or Dante or Michaelangelo in the 1300s, but by Giacomo di Lentino in Sicily in the late 1200s. The Lentinian or Sicilian Sonnet (derived from the eight-line Strambotto) uses the Sicilian Octave: **abababab** followed by a Sicilian Sestet: **cdcdcd**. Petrarch's classic Italian Octave: **abbaabba** marks the standard for the Italian/Petrarchan sonnet (**abbaabba ‖ cdcdcd** OR **cdecde**; second, I believe we must consider any 14-line poem to be a sonnet.

Modern English is, despite being the largest language in number of words of any language ever used, is "rhyme poor"—due to our grammatical dropping of case endings and most inflections, making English a syntactical language.

Sir Thomas Wyatt didn't simplify the issue with his sonnet—except breaking the Italian taboo against ending the sonnet with a couplet. Both he and John Donne and others used: **abbaabba cddcee** .

Henry Howard, Earl of Surrey, was the real rebel and his English (should really be called "Surreyan," but "Shakespearean" pre-empted the optional name) is much simpler to rhyme in English: **abab cdcd efef gg**. This, of course, also broke the "sense division" of the poem into 4-4-4-2 segments rather than the 8-6/octave-sestet of the Sicilian, Italian, and Wyatt forms.

But good old Edmund Spenser came along and recomplicated the English sonnet by interlocking the rhymes of the quatrains: **abab bcbc cdcd ee**—just as hard to rhyme as the earlier forms!

It would be very had to count the number of experiments since. But, as I've said: We should consider any quatorzain to be a sonnet of some sort.

Sonetto Rispetto: The Sonetto Rispetto uses Ottava Rima for its octave: ababacc. This is followed by either the Italian Sestet [cdecde] or the Sicillian Sestet [cdcdcd].

Stornello [Sonnet]*: The Italian form of the Stornello is written in triplets, but with the middle line slant or near-rhyming (not full-rhyming) with the enveloping other two. So **AaA BbB CcC**, etc. I've added a rhymed couplet to four Stornello triplets to make a **Stornello [Sonnet]**.

TELESILLEAN METRE: is named for the woman poet Telesilla of Argos (5th c. BC). It is Actually an acephalous ("headless"/first syllable removed) Glyconic line running in accentual-syllabic approximation as an Iamb, a Dactyl and an Amphimacer: u/ /uu /u/ The first foot may be a Spondee //. I have used this in rhymed couplets for my **TELESILLEAN SONNET** and sought to approximate the flow of the meter.

TERCETINA* [**TERCETINA SONNET***]: My invented forms, based upon the mathmatical arrangements of the Sestina. Exact end words MAY be repeated, as in the true sestina, but rhymed words may be used instead.

The first four sections of the **TERCETINA SONNET*** form a proper ten-line **TERCETINA.*** The pattern of repeated words (or rhymes) is: 123 312 231 [123] / **abc cab bca [abc]** where the last group are words/rhymes falling in a single, separate line. Hence: the look on the page is 3-3-3-1 lines.

The last four lines of the **TERCETINA SONNET*** rhyme 4554 / **deed**
For these forms, lengths of lines and types of meter are optional.

TERZA RIMA [**TERZA RIMA SONNET**]: Terza Rima ("rhyme in threes") is the classic interlocking tercet pattern used by Dante in the three books of his *The Divine Comedy.* The form makes possible poems of extensive length, as well as providing a challenge for the rhymer. The pattern is **aba bcb cdc ded, etc.** Such poems or sections of a poem in this meter usually end with *either* a couplet or a triplet to close out the poem, sometimes picking up the initial rhyme of the first stanza as the middle of a final tercet. The **TERZA RIMA SONNET** rhymes: aba bcb cdc ded ee, for 14.

WEBB'S SONNET*: This is a sonnet form suggested by my friend and fellow poet, Don Webb in a Facebook discussion. The scheme he suggested is a quatrain **abab** followed by a reflexive group of ten lines: **cdefggfedc**

A challange *proving that content may follow form.* This quickly suggested a mirror to me—resulting in my poem, "The Unlikeness" (p. 137).

COLPHON

THE COVER TITLE & SECTION DIVISIONS ARE SET IN DESDEMONA IN VARIOUS SIZES

The Emphasis Text is set in William Morris' Golden Type (Golden Type ITC Std) in various weights from Black to Bold to Regular Also used for Poem Titles

The basic body copy text is 13 point Adobe Jenson Pro
set on 15 points or 15.6 with various point sizes
for the epigraphsand for type-of-poem identifiers

Copyright 31 May 2021

Lightning Source UK Ltd.
Milton Keynes UK
UKHW041333130123
415271UK00025B/31